I0682526

SUSY,

A STORY OF THE PLAINS

BRET HARTE

1st WORLD
LIBRARY
Literary Society

Susy, A Story of the Plains

Bret Harte

© 1st World Library, 2009
PO Box 2211
Fairfield, IA 52556
www.1stworldlibrary.com
First Edition

LCCN: 2009923371

Softcover ISBN: 978-1-4218-8816-3
Hardcover ISBN: 978-1-4218-8915-3
eBook ISBN: 978-1-4218-8717-3

Purchase *"Susy, A Story of the Plains"*
as a traditional bound book at:
www.1stWorldLibrary.com/purchase.asp?ISBN=978-1-4218-8816-3

1st World Library is a literary, educational organization
dedicated to:

- Creating a free internet library of downloadable ebooks

- Hosting writing competitions and offering book publishing
scholarships.

Interested in more 1st World Library books? contact:
literacy@1stworldlibrary.com
Check us out at: www.1stworldlibrary.com

1st World Library Literary Society

Giving Back to the World

"If you want to work on the core problem, it's early school literacy."

- James Barksdale, former CEO of Netscape

"No skill is more crucial to the future of a child, or to a democratic and prosperous society, than literacy."

- Los Angeles Times

"Literacy... means far more than learning how to read and write... The aim is to transmit... knowledge and promote social participation."

- UNESCO

"Literacy is not a luxury, it is a right and a responsibility. If our world is to meet the challenges of the twenty-first century we must harness the energy and creativity of all our citizens."

- President Bill Clinton

"Parents should be encouraged to read to their children, and teachers should be equipped with all available techniques for teaching literacy, so the varying needs and capacities of individual kids can be taken into account."

- Hugh Mackay

CHAPTER I

Where the San Leandro turnpike stretches its dusty, hot, and interminable length along the valley, at a point where the heat and dust have become intolerable, the monotonous expanse of wild oats on either side illimitable, and the distant horizon apparently remoter than ever, it suddenly slips between a stunted thicket or hedge of "scrub oaks," which until that moment had been undistinguishable above the long, misty, quivering level of the grain. The thicket rising gradually in height, but with a regular slope whose gradient had been determined by centuries of western trade winds, presently becomes a fair wood of live-oak, and a few hundred yards further at last assumes the aspect of a primeval forest. A delicious coolness fills the air; the long, shadowy aisles greet the aching eye with a soothing twilight; the murmur of unseen brooks is heard, and, by a strange irony, the enormous, widely-spaced stacks of wild oats are replaced by a carpet of tiny-leaved mosses and chickweed at the roots of trees, and the minutest clover in more open spaces. The baked and cracked adobe soil of the now vanished plains is exchanged for a heavy red mineral dust and gravel, rocks and boulders make their appearance, and at times the road is crossed by the white veins of quartz. It is still the San Leandro turnpike—a few miles later to rise from this canada into the upper plains again—but it is also the actual gateway and avenue to the Robles Rancho. When the departing visitors of Judge Peyton, now owner of the rancho, reach the outer plains again, after twenty minutes' drive from the house, the canada, rancho, and avenue have as completely disappeared from view as if they had been swallowed up in the plain.

A cross road from the turnpike is the usual approach to the casa or mansion—a long, low quadrangle of brown adobe wall in a bare but gently sloping eminence. And here a second surprise meets the stranger. He seems to have emerged from the forest upon another illimitable plain, but one utterly trackless, wild, and desolate. It is, however, only a lower terrace of the same valley, and, in fact, comprises the three square leagues of the Robles Rancho. Uncultivated and savage as it appears, given over to wild cattle and horses that sometimes sweep in frightened bands around the very casa itself, the long south wall of the corral embraces an orchard of gnarled pear-trees, an old vineyard, and a venerable garden of olives and oranges. A manor, formerly granted by Charles V. to Don Vincente Robles, of Andalusia, of pious and ascetic memory, it had commended itself to Judge Peyton, of Kentucky, a modern heretic pioneer of bookish tastes and secluded habits, who had bought it of Don Vincente's descendants. Here Judge Peyton seemed to have realized his idea of a perfect climate, and a retirement, half-studious, half-active, with something of the seignioralty of the old slaveholder that he had been. Here, too, he had seen the hope of restoring his wife's health—for which he had undertaken the overland emigration—more than fulfilled in Mrs. Peyton's improved physical condition, albeit at the expense, perhaps, of some of the languorous graces of ailing American wifehood.

It was with a curious recognition of this latter fact that Judge Peyton watched his wife crossing the patio or courtyard with her arm around the neck of her adopted daughter "Suzette."

A sudden memory crossed his mind of the first day that he had seen them together—the day that he had brought the child and her boy-companion—two estrays from an emigrant train on the plains—to his wife in camp. Certainly Mrs. Peyton was stouter and stronger fibred; the wonderful Californian climate had materialized her figure, as it had their Eastern fruits and flowers, but it was stranger that "Susy"—the child of homelier frontier blood and parentage, whose wholesome peasant plumpness had at first attracted them—should have grown thinner and more graceful, and even seemed to have gained the delicacy his wife had lost. Six years had imperceptibly wrought this change; it had never struck him before so forcibly as on this day of Susy's return from the convent school at Santa Clara for the holidays.

The woman and child had reached the broad veranda which, on one side of the patio, replaced the old Spanish corridor. It was the single modern innovation that Peyton had allowed himself when he had broken the quadrangular symmetry of the old house with a wooden "annexe" or addition beyond the walls. It made a pleasant lounging-place, shadowed from the hot midday sun by sloping roofs and awnings, and sheltered from the boisterous afternoon trade winds by the opposite side of the court. But Susy did not seem inclined to linger there long that morning, in spite of Mrs. Peyton's evident desire for a maternal tete-a-tete. The nervous preoccupation and capricious ennui of an indulged child showed in her pretty but discontented face, and knit her curved eyebrows, and Peyton saw a look of pain pass over his wife's face as the young girl suddenly and half-laughingly broke away and fluttered off towards the old garden.

Mrs. Peyton looked up and caught her husband's eye.

"I am afraid Susy finds it more dull here every time she

returns," she said, with an apologetic smile. "I am glad she has invited one of her school friends to come for a visit tomorrow. You know, yourself, John," she added, with a slight partisan attitude, "that the lonely old house and wild plain are not particularly lively for young people, however much they may suit YOUR ways."

"It certainly must be dull if she can't stand it for three weeks in the year," said her husband dryly. "But we really cannot open the San Francisco house for her summer vacation, nor can we move from the rancho to a more fashionable locality. Besides, it will do her good to run wild here. I can remember when she wasn't so fastidious. In fact, I was thinking just now how changed she was from the day when we picked her up"—

"How often am I to remind you, John," interrupted the lady, with some impatience, "that we agreed never to speak of her past, or even to think of her as anything but our own child. You know how it pains me! And the poor dear herself has forgotten it, and thinks of us only as her own parents. I really believe that if that wretched father and mother of hers had not been killed by the Indians, or were to come to life again, she would neither know them nor care for them. I mean, of course, John," she said, averting her eyes from a slightly cynical smile on her husband's face, "that it's only natural for young children to be forgetful, and ready to take new impressions."

"And as long, dear, as WE are not the subjects of this youthful forgetfulness, and she isn't really finding US as stupid as the rancho," replied her husband cheerfully, "I suppose we mustn't complain."

"John, how can you talk such nonsense?" said Mrs. Peyton impatiently. "But I have no fear of that," she added, with a slightly ostentatious confidence. "I only wish I was as sure"—

"Of what?"

"Of nothing happening that could take her from us. I do not mean death, John—like our first little one. That does not happen to one twice; but I sometimes dread"—

"What? She's only fifteen, and it's rather early to think about the only other inevitable separation—marriage. Come, Ally, this is mere fancy. She has been given up to us by her family —at least, by all that we know are left of them. I have legally adopted her. If I have not made her my heiress, it is because I prefer to leave everything to YOU, and I would rather she should know that she was dependent upon you for the future than upon me."

"And I can make a will in her favor if I want to?" said Mrs. Peyton quickly.

"Always," responded her husband smilingly; "but you have ample time to think of that, I trust. Meanwhile I have some news for you which may make Susy's visit to the rancho this time less dull to her. You remember Clarence Brant, the boy who was with her when we picked her up, and who really saved her life?"

"No, I don't," said Mrs. Peyton pettishly, "nor do I want to! You know, John, how distasteful and unpleasant it is for me to have those dreary, petty, and vulgar details of the poor child's past life recalled, and, thank Heaven, I have forgotten them except when you choose to drag them before me. You agreed, long ago, that we were never to talk of the Indian massacre of her parents, so that we could also ignore it before her; then why do you talk of her vulgar friends, who are just as unpleasant? Please let us drop the past."

"Willingly, my dear; but, unfortunately, we cannot make others do it. And this is a case in point. It appears that this boy, whom we brought to Sacramento to deliver to a relative"—

"And who was a wicked little impostor—you remember that yourself, John, for he said that he was the son of Colonel Brant, and that he was dead; and you know, and my brother Harry knew, that Colonel Brant was alive all the time, and that he was lying, and Colonel Brant was not his father," broke in Mrs. Peyton impatiently.

"As it seems you do remember that much," said Peyton dryly, "it is only just to him that I should tell you that it appears that he was not an impostor. His story was TRUE. I have just learned that Colonel Brant WAS actually his father, but had concealed his lawless life here, as well as his identity, from the boy. He was really that vague relative to whom Clarence was confided, and under that disguise he afterwards protected the boy, had him carefully educated at the Jesuit College of San Jose, and, dying two years ago in that filibuster raid in Mexico, left him a considerable fortune."

"And what has he to do with Susy's holidays?" said Mrs. Peyton, with uneasy quickness. "John, you surely cannot expect her ever to meet this common creature again, with his vulgar ways. His wretched associates like that Jim Hooker, and, as you yourself admit, the blood of an assassin, duelist, and—Heaven knows what kind of a pirate his father wasn't at the last—in his veins! You don't believe that a lad of this type, however much of his father's ill-gotten money he may have, can be fit company for your daughter? You never could have thought of inviting him here?"

"I'm afraid that's exactly what I have done, Ally," said the smiling but unmoved Peyton; "but I'm still more afraid that your conception of his present condition is an unfair one, like your remembrance of his past. Father Sobriente, whom I met at San Jose yesterday, says he is very intelligent, and thoroughly educated, with charming manners and refined tastes. His father's money, which they say was an investment for him in Carson's Bank five years ago, is as good as any one's, and his father's blood won't hurt him in California or the Southwest. At least, he is received everywhere, and Don Juan Robinson was his guardian. Indeed, as far as social status goes, it might be a serious question if the actual daughter of the late John Silsbee, of Pike County, and the adopted child of John Peyton was in the least his superior. As Father Sobriente evidently knew Clarence's former companionship with Susy and her parents, it would be hardly politic for us to ignore it or seem to be ashamed of it. So I entrusted Sobriente with an invitation to young Brant on the spot."

Mrs. Peyton's impatience, indignation, and opposition, which had successively given way before her husband's quiet, masterful good humor, here took the form of a neurotic fatalism. She shook her head with superstitious resignation.

"Didn't I tell you, John, that I always had a dread of something coming"—

"But if it comes in the shape of a shy young lad, I see nothing singularly portentous in it. They have not met since they were quite small; their tastes have changed; if they don't quarrel and fight they may be equally bored with each other. Yet until then, in one way or another, Clarence will occupy the young lady's vacant caprice, and her school friend, Mary Rogers, will be here, you know, to divide his attentions, and," added Peyton, with mock solemnity, "preserve the interest of strict propriety. Shall I break it to her—or will you?"

"No—yes," hesitated Mrs. Peyton; "perhaps I had better."

"Very well, I leave his character in your hands; only don't prejudice her into a romantic fancy for him." And Judge Peyton lounged smilingly away.

Then two little tears forced themselves from Mrs. Peyton's eyes. Again she saw that prospect of uninterrupted companionship with Susy, upon which each successive year she had built so many maternal hopes and confidences, fade away before her. She dreaded the coming of Susy's school friend, who shared her daughter's present thoughts and intimacy, although she had herself invited her in a more desperate dread of the child's abstracted, discontented eyes; she dreaded the advent of the boy who had shared Susy's early life before she knew her; she dreaded the ordeal of breaking the news and perhaps seeing that pretty animation spring into her eyes, which she had begun to believe no solicitude or tenderness of her own ever again awakened— and yet she dreaded still more that her husband should see it too. For the love of this recreated woman, although not entirely materialized with her changed fibre, had nevertheless become a coarser selfishness fostered by her loneliness and limited experience. The maternal yearning left unsatisfied by the loss of her first-born had never been filled by Susy's thoughtless acceptance of it; she had been led astray by the child's easy transference of dependence and the forgetfulness of youth, and was only now dimly conscious of finding herself face to face with an alien nature.

She started to her feet and followed the direction that Susy had taken. For a moment she had to front the afternoon trade wind which chilled her as it swept the plain beyond the gateway, but was stopped by the adobe wall, above whose shelter the stunted treetops—through years of exposure—slanted as if trimmed by gigantic shears. At first, looking down the venerable alley of fantastic, knotted shapes, she saw no trace of Susy. But half way down the gleam of a white skirt against a thicket of dark olives showed her the young girl sitting on a bench in a neglected arbor. In the midst of this formal and faded pageantry she looked charmingly fresh, youthful, and pretty; and yet the unfortunate woman thought that her attitude and expression at that moment suggested more than her fifteen years of girlhood. Her golden hair still hung unfettered over her straight, boy-like back and shoulders; her short skirt still showed her childish feet and ankles; yet there seemed to be some undefined maturity or a vague womanliness about her that stung Mrs. Peyton's heart. The child was growing away from her, too!

"Susy!"

The young girl raised her head quickly; her deep violet eyes seemed also to leap with a sudden suspicion, and with a half-mechanical, secretive movement, that might have been only a schoolgirl's instinct, her right hand had slipped a paper on which she was scribbling between the leaves of her book. Yet the next moment, even while looking interrogatively at her mother, she withdrew the paper quietly, tore it up into small pieces, and threw them on the ground.

But Mrs. Peyton was too preoccupied with her news to notice the circumstance, and too nervous in her haste to be tactful. "Susy, your father has invited that boy, Clarence Brant—you know that creature we picked up and assisted on the plains, when you were a mere baby—to come down here and make us a visit."

Her heart seemed to stop beating as she gazed breathlessly at the girl. But Susy's face, unchanged except for the alert, questioning eyes, remained fixed for a moment; then a childish smile of wonder opened her small red mouth, expanded it slightly as she said simply:—

"Lor, mar! He hasn't, really!"

Inexpressibly, yet unreasonably reassured, Mrs. Peyton hurriedly recounted her husband's story of Clarence's fortune, and was even joyfully surprised into some fairness of statement.

"But you don't remember him much, do you, dear? It was so long ago, and—you are quite a young lady now," she added eagerly.

The open mouth was still fixed; the wondering smile would have been idiotic in any face less dimpled, rosy, and piquant than Susy's. After a slight gasp, as if in still incredulous and partly reminiscent preoccupation, she said without replying:—

"How funny! When is he coming?"

"Day after to-morrow," returned Mrs. Peyton, with a contented smile.

"And Mary Rogers will be here, too. It will be real fun for her."

Mrs. Peyton was more than reassured. Half ashamed of her jealous fears, she drew Susy's golden head towards her and kissed it. And the young girl, still reminiscent, with smilingly abstracted toleration, returned the caress.

CHAPTER II

It was not thought inconsistent with Susy's capriciousness that she should declare her intention the next morning of driving her pony buggy to Santa Inez to anticipate the stage-coach and fetch Mary Rogers from the station. Mrs. Peyton, as usual, supported the young lady's whim and opposed her husband's objections.

"Because the stage-coach happens to pass our gate, John, it is no reason why Susy shouldn't drive her friend from Santa Inez if she prefers it. It's only seven miles, and you can send Pedro to follow her on horseback to see that she comes to no harm."

"But that isn't Pedro's business," said Peyton.

"He ought to be proud of the privilege," returned the lady, with a toss of her head.

Peyton smiled grimly, but yielded; and when the stage-coach drew up the next afternoon at the Santa Inez Hotel, Susy was already waiting in her pony carriage before it. Although the susceptible driver, expressman, and passengers generally, charmed with this golden-haired vision, would have gladly protracted the meeting of the two young friends, the transfer of Mary Rogers from the coach to the carriage was effected with considerable hauteur and youthful dignity by Susy. Even Mary Rogers, two years Susy's senior, a serious brunette, whose good-humor did not, however, impair her capacity for sentiment, was impressed and even embarrassed by her demeanor; but only for a moment. When they had driven from the hotel and were fairly hidden again in the dust of the outlying plain, with the discreet Pedro hovering in the distance, Susy dropped the reins, and, grasping her companion's arm, gasped, in tones of dramatic intensity:—

"He's been heard from, and is coming HERE!"

"Who?"

A sickening sense that her old confidante had already lost touch with her—they had been separated for nearly two weeks—might have passed through Susy's mind.

"Who?" she repeated, with a vicious shake of Mary's arm, "why, Clarence Brant, of course."

"No!" said Mary, vaguely.

Nevertheless, Susy went on rapidly, as if to neutralize the effect of her comrade's vacuity.

"You never could have imagined it! Never! Even I, when mother told me, I thought I should have fainted, and ALL would have been revealed!"

"But," hesitated the still wondering confidante, "I thought that was all over long ago. You haven't seen him nor heard from him since that day you met accidentally at Santa Clara, two years ago, have you?"

Susy's eyes shot a blue ray of dark but unutterable

significance into Mary's, and then were carefully averted. Mary Rogers, although perfectly satisfied that Susy had never seen Clarence since, nevertheless instantly accepted and was even thrilled with this artful suggestion of a clandestine correspondence. Such was the simple faith of youthful friendship.

"Mother knows nothing of it, of course, and a word from you or him would ruin everything," continued the breathless Susy. "That's why I came to fetch you and warn you. You must see him first, and warn him at any cost. If I hadn't run every risk to come here to-day, Heaven knows what might have happened! What do you think of the ponies, dear? They're my own, and the sweetest! This one's Susy, that one Clarence—but privately, you know. Before the world and in the stables he's only Birdie."

"But I thought you wrote to me that you called them 'Paul and Virginie,'" said Mary doubtfully.

"I do, sometimes," said Susy calmly. "But one has to learn to suppress one's feelings, dear!" Then quickly, "I do so hate deceit, don't you? Tell me, don't you think deceit perfectly hateful?"

Without waiting for her friend's loyal assent, she continued rapidly: "And he's just rolling in wealth! and educated, papa says, to the highest degree!"

"Then," began Mary, "if he's coming with your mother's consent, and if you haven't quarreled, and it is not broken off, I should think you'd be just delighted."

But another quick flash from Susy's eyes dispersed these beatific visions of the future. "Hush!" she said, with suppressed dramatic intensity. "You know not what you say!

There's an awful mystery hangs over him. Mary Rogers," continued the young girl, approaching her small mouth to her confidante's ear in an appalling whisper. "His father was—a PIRATE! Yes—lived a pirate and was killed a pirate!"

The statement, however, seemed to be partly ineffective. Mary Rogers was startled but not alarmed, and even protested feebly. "But," she said, "if the father's dead, what's that to do with Clarence? He was always with your papa—so you told me, dear—or other people, and couldn't catch anything from his own father. And I'm sure, dearest, he always seemed nice and quiet."

"Yes, SEEMED," returned Susy darkly, "but that's all you know! It was in his BLOOD. You know it always is—you read it in the books—you could see it in his eye. There were times, my dear, when he was thwarted—when the slightest attention from another person to me revealed it! I have kept it to myself—but think, dearest, of the effects of jealousy on that passionate nature! Sometimes I tremble to look back upon it."

Nevertheless, she raised her hands and threw back her lovely golden mane from her childish shoulders with an easy, untroubled gesture. It was singular that Mary Rogers, leaning back comfortably in the buggy, also accepted these heart-rending revelations with comfortably knitted brows and luxuriously contented concern. If she found it difficult to recognize in the picture just drawn by Susy the quiet, gentle, and sadly reserved youth she had known, she said nothing. After a silence, lazily watching the distant wheeling vacquero, she said:—

"And your father always sends an outrider like that with you? How nice! So picturesque—and like the old Spanish days."

"Hush!" said Susy, with another unutterable glance.

But this time Mary was in full sympathetic communion with her friend, and equal to any incoherent hiatus of revelation.

"No!" she said promptly, "you don't mean it!"

"Don't ask me, I daren't say anything to papa, for he'd be simply furious. But there are times when we're alone, and Pedro wheels down so near with SUCH a look in his black eyes, that I'm all in a tremble. It's dreadful! They say he's a real Briones—and he sometimes says something in Spanish, ending with 'senorita,' but I pretend I don't understand."

"And I suppose that if anything should happen to the ponies, he'd just risk his life to save you."

"Yes—and it would be so awful—for I just hate him!"

"But if I was with you, dear, he couldn't expect you to be as grateful as if you were alone. Susy!" she continued after a pause, "if you just stirred up the ponies a little so as to make 'em go fast, perhaps he might think they'd got away from you, and come dashing down here. It would be so funny to see him—wouldn't it?"

The two girls looked at each other; their eyes sparkled already with a fearful joy—they drew a long breath of guilty anticipation. For a moment Susy even believed in her imaginary sketch of Pedro's devotion.

"Papa said I wasn't to use the whip except in a case of necessity," she said, reaching for the slender silver-handled toy, and setting her pretty lips together with the added determination of disobedience. "G'long!"—and she laid the lash smartly on the shining backs of the animals.

They were wiry, slender brutes of Mojave Indian blood, only lately broken to harness, and still undisciplined in temper. The lash sent them rearing into the air, where, forgetting themselves in the slackened traces and loose reins, they came down with a succession of bounds that brought the light buggy leaping after them with its wheels scarcely touching the ground. That unlucky lash had knocked away the bonds of a few months' servitude and sent the half-broken brutes instinctively careering with arched backs and kicking heels into the field towards the nearest cover.

Mary Rogers cast a hurried glance over her shoulder. Alas, they had not calculated on the insidious levels of the terraced plain, and the faithful Pedro had suddenly disappeared; the intervention of six inches of rising wild oats had wiped him out of the prospect and their possible salvation as completely as if he had been miles away. Nevertheless, the girls were not frightened; perhaps they had not time. There was, how-ever, the briefest interval for the most dominant of feminine emotions, and it was taken advantage of by Susy.

"It was all YOUR fault, dear!" she gasped, as the forewheels of the buggy, dropping into a gopher rut, suddenly tilted up the back of the vehicle and shot its fair occupants into the yielding palisades of dusty grain. The shock detached the whiffletree from the splinter-bar, snapped the light pole, and, turning the now thoroughly frightened animals again from their course, sent them, goaded by the clattering fragments, flying down the turnpike. Half a mile farther on they overtook the gleaming white canvas hood of a slowly moving wagon drawn by two oxen, and, swerving again, the nearer pony stepped upon a trailing trace and ingloriously ended their career by rolling himself and his companion in the dust at the very feet of the peacefully plodding team.

Equally harmless and inglorious was the catastrophe of Susy

and her friend. The strong, elastic stalks of the tall grain broke their fall and enabled them to scramble to their feet, dusty, disheveled, but unhurt, and even unstunned by the shock. Their first instinctive cries over a damaged hat or ripped skirt were followed by the quick reaction of childish laughter. They were alone; the very defection of Pedro consoled them, in its absence of any witness to their disaster; even their previous slight attitude to each other was forgotten. They groped their way, pushing and panting, to the road again, where, beholding the overset buggy with its wheels ludicrously in the air, they suddenly seized and shook each other, and in an outburst of hilarious ecstasy, fairly laughed until the tears came into their eyes.

Then there was a breathless silence.

"The stage will be coming by in a moment," composedly said Susy. "Fix me, dear."

Mary Rogers calmly walked around her friend, bestowing a practical shake there, a pluck here, completely retying one bow and restoring an engaging fullness to another, yet critically examining, with her head on one side, the fascinating result. Then Susy performed the same function for Mary with equal deliberation and deftness. Suddenly Mary started and looked up.

"It's coming," she said quickly, "and they've SEEN US."

The expression of the faces of the two girls instantly changed. A pained dignity and resignation, apparently born of the most harrowing experiences and controlled only by perfect good breeding, was distinctly suggested in their features and attitude as they stood patiently by the wreck of their overturned buggy awaiting the oncoming coach. In sharp contrast was the evident excitement among the passengers. A few rose from their seats in their eagerness; as the stage pulled up in the road beside the buggy four or five of the younger men leaped to the ground.

"Are you hurt, miss?" they gasped sympathetically.

Susy did not immediately reply, but ominously knitted her pretty eyebrows as if repressing a spasm of pain. Then she said, "Not at all," coldly, with the suggestion of stoically concealing some lasting or perhaps fatal injury, and took the arm of Mary Rogers, who had, in the mean time, established a touching yet graceful limp.

Declining the proffered assistance of the passengers, they helped each other into the coach, and freezingly requesting the driver to stop at Mr. Peyton's gate, maintained a statuesque and impressive silence. At the gates they got down, followed by the sympathetic glances of the others.

To all appearance their escapade, albeit fraught with dangerous possibilities, had happily ended. But in the economy of human affairs, as in nature, forces are not suddenly let loose without more or less sympathetic disturbance which is apt to linger after the impelling cause is harmlessly spent. The fright which the girls had unsuccessfully attempted to produce in the heart of their escort had passed him to become a panic elsewhere. Judge Peyton, riding near the gateway of his rancho, was suddenly confronted by the spectacle of one of his vacqueros driving on before him the two lassoed and dusty ponies, with a face that broke into violent gesticulating at his master's quick interrogation.

"Ah! Mother of God! It was an evil day! For the bronchos had run away, upset the buggy, and had only been stopped by a brave Americano of an ox-team, whose lasso was even now around their necks, to prove it, and who had been dragged a matter of a hundred varas, like a calf, at their heels. The senoritas—ah! had he not already said they were safe, by the mercy of Jesus!—picked up by the coach, and would be here at this moment."

"But where was Pedro all the time? What was he doing?" demanded Peyton, with a darkened face and gathering anger.

The vacquero looked at his master, and shrugged his shoulders significantly. At any other time Peyton would have remembered that Pedro, as the reputed scion of a decayed Spanish family, and claiming superiority, was not a favorite with his fellow-retainers. But the gesture, half of suggestion, half of depreciation, irritated Peyton still more.

"Well, where is this American who DID something when there wasn't a man among you all able to stop a child's runaway ponies?" he said sarcastically. "Let me see him."

The vacquero became still more deprecatory.

"Ah! He had driven on with his team towards San Antonio. He would not stop to be thanked. But that was the whole truth. He, Incarnacion, could swear to it as to the Creed. There was nothing more."

"Take those beasts around the back way to the corral," said Peyton, thoroughly enraged, "and not a word of this to any one at the casa, do you hear? Not a word to Mrs. Peyton or the servants, or, by Heaven, I'll clear the rancho of the whole lazy crew of you at once. Out of the way there, and be off!"

He spurred his horse past the frightened menial, and dashed down the narrow lane that led to the gate. But, as Incarnacion had truly said, "It was an evil day," for at the bottom of the lane, ambling slowly along as he lazily puffed a yellow cigarette, appeared the figure of the erring Pedro. Utterly unconscious of the accident, attributing the disappearance of his charges to the inequalities of the plain, and, in truth, little interested in what he firmly believed was his purely artificial function, he had even made a larger circuit to stop at a wayside fonda for refreshments.

Unfortunately, there is no more illogical sequence of human emotion than the exasperation produced by the bland manner of the unfortunate object who has excited it, although that very unconcern may be the convincing proof of innocence of intention. Judge Peyton, already influenced, was furious at the comfortable obliviousness of his careless henchman, and rode angrily towards him. Only a quick turn of Pedro's wrist kept the two men from coming into collision.

"Is this the way you attend to your duty?" demanded Peyton, in a thick, suppressed voice, "Where is the buggy? Where is my daughter?"

There was no mistaking Judge Peyton's manner, even if the reason of it was not so clear to Pedro's mind, and his hot Latin blood flew instinctively to his face. But for that, he might have shown some concern or asked an explanation. As it was, he at once retorted with the national shrug and the national half-scornful, half-lazy "Quien sabe?"

"Who knows?" repeated Peyton, hotly. "I do! She was thrown out of her buggy through your negligence and infernal laziness! The ponies ran away, and were stopped by a stranger who wasn't afraid of risking his bones, while you were limping around somewhere like a slouching, cowardly coyote."

The vacquero struggled a moment between blank astonishment and inarticulate rage. At last he burst out:—

Bret Harte

"I am no coyote! I was there! I saw no runaway!"

"Don't lie to me, sir!" roared Peyton. "I tell you the buggy was smashed, the girls were thrown out and nearly killed"— He stopped suddenly. The sound of youthful laughter had come from the bottom of the lane, where Susy Peyton and Mary Rogers, just alighted from the coach, in the reaction of their previous constrained attitude, were flying hilariously into view. A slight embarrassment crossed Peyton's face; a still deeper flush of anger overspread Pedro's sullen cheek.

Then Pedro found tongue again, his native one, rapidly, violently, half incoherently. "Ah, yes! It had come to this. It seems he was not a vacquero, a companion of the padrone on lands that had been his own before the Americanos robbed him of it, but a servant, a lackey of muchachas, an attendant on children to amuse them, or—why not?—an appendage to his daughter's state! Ah, Jesus Maria! such a state! such a muchacha! A picked-up foundling—a swineherd's daughter —to be ennobled by his, Pedro's, attendance, and for whose vulgar, clownish tricks—tricks of a swineherd's daughter— he, Pedro, was to be brought to book and insulted as if she were of Hidalgo blood! Ah, Caramba! Don Juan Peyton would find he could no more make a servant of him than he could make a lady of her!"

The two young girls were rapidly approaching. Judge Peyton spurred his horse beside the vacquero's, and, swinging the long thong of his bridle ominously in his clenched fingers, said, with a white face:—

"Vamos!"

Pedro's hand slid towards his sash. Peyton only looked at him with a rigid smile of scorn.

"Or I'll lash you here before them both," he added in a lower voice.

The vacquero met Peyton's relentless eyes with a yellow flash of hate, drew his reins sharply, until his mustang, galled by the cruel bit, reared suddenly as if to strike at the immovable American, then, apparently with the same action, he swung it around on its hind legs, as on a pivot, and dashed towards the corral at a furious gallop.

CHAPTER III

Meantime the heroic proprietor of the peaceful ox-team, whose valor Incarnacion had so infelicitously celebrated, was walking listlessly in the dust beside his wagon. At a first glance his slouching figure, taken in connection with his bucolic conveyance, did not immediately suggest a hero. As he emerged from the dusty cloud it could be seen that he was wearing a belt from which a large dragoon revolver and hunting knife were slung, and placed somewhat ostentatiously across the wagon seat was a rifle. Yet the other contents of the wagon were of a singularly inoffensive character, and even suggested articles of homely barter. Culinary utensils of all sizes, tubs, scullery brushes, and clocks, with several rolls of cheap carpeting and calico, might have been the wares of some traveling vender. Yet, as they were only visible through a flap of the drawn curtains of the canvas hood, they did not mitigate the general aggressive effect of their owner's appearance. A red bandanna handkerchief knotted and thrown loosely over his shoulders, a slouched hat pulled darkly over a head of long tangled hair, which, however, shadowed a round, comfortable face, scantily and youthfully bearded, were part of these confusing inconsistencies.

The shadows of the team wagon were already lengthening grotesquely over the flat, cultivated fields, which for some time had taken the place of the plains of wild oats in the branch road into which they had turned. The gigantic shadow of the proprietor, occasionally projected before it, was in characteristic exaggeration, and was often obliterated by a puff of dust, stirred by the plodding hoofs of the peaceful oxen, and swept across the field by the strong afternoon trades. The sun sank lower, although a still potent presence above the horizon line; the creaking wagon lumbered still heavily along. Yet at intervals its belligerent proprietor would start up from his slouching, silent march, break out into violent, disproportionate, but utterly ineffective objurgation of his cattle, jump into the air and kick his heels together in some paroxysm of indignation against them—an act, however, which was received always with heavy bovine indifference, the dogged scorn of swaying, repudiating heads, or the dull contempt of lazily flicking tails.

Towards sunset one or two straggling barns and cottages indicated their approach to the outskirts of a country town or settlement. Here the team halted, as if the belligerent-looking teamster had felt his appearance was inconsistent with an effeminate civilization, and the oxen were turned into an open waste opposite a nondescript wooden tenement, half farmhouse and half cabin, evidently of the rudest Western origin. He may have recognized the fact that these "shanties" were not, as the ordinary traveler might infer, the first rude shelter of the original pioneers or settlers, but the later makeshifts of some recent Western immigrants who, like himself, probably found themselves unequal to the settled habits of the village, and who still retained their nomadic instincts. It chanced, however, that the cabin at present was occupied by a New England mechanic and his family, who had emigrated by ship around Cape Horn, and who had no experience of the West, the plains, or its people. It was therefore with some curiosity and a certain amount of fascinated awe that the mechanic's only daughter regarded from the open door of her dwelling the arrival of this wild and lawless-looking stranger.

Meantime he had opened the curtains of the wagon and taken from its interior a number of pots, pans, and culinary utensils, which he proceeded to hang upon certain hooks that were placed on the outer ribs of the board and the sides of the vehicle. To this he added a roll of rag carpet, the end of which hung from the tailboard, and a roll of pink calico temptingly displayed on the seat. The mystification and curiosity of the young girl grew more intense at these proceedings. It looked like the ordinary exhibition of a traveling peddler, but the gloomy and embattled appearance of the man himself scouted so peaceful and commonplace a suggestion. Under the pretense of chasing away a marauding hen, she sallied out upon the waste near the wagon. It then became evident that the traveler had seen her, and was not averse to her interest in his movements, although he had not changed his attitude of savage retrospection. An occasional ejaculation of suppressed passion, as if the memory of some past conflict was too much for him, escaped him even in this peaceful occupation. As this possibly caused the young girl to still hover timidly in the distance, he suddenly entered the wagon and reappeared carrying a tin bucket, with which he somewhat ostentatiously crossed her path, his eyes darkly wandering as if seeking something.

"If you're lookin' for the spring, it's a spell furder on—by the willows."

It was a pleasant voice, the teamster thought, albeit with a dry, crisp, New England accent unfamiliar to his ears. He looked into the depths of an unlovely blue-check sunbonnet, and saw certain small, irregular features and a sallow check, lit up by a pair of perfectly innocent, trustful, and wondering brown eyes. Their timid possessor seemed to be a girl of seventeen, whose figure, although apparently clad in one of her mother's gowns, was still undeveloped and repressed by rustic hardship and innutrition. As her eyes met his she saw that the face of this gloomy stranger was still youthful, by no means implacable, and, even at that moment, was actually suffused by a brick-colored blush! In matters of mere intuition, the sex, even in its most rustic phase, is still our superior; and this unsophisticated girl, as the trespasser stammered, "Thank ye, miss," was instinctively emboldened to greater freedom.

"Dad ain't tu hum, but ye kin have a drink o' milk if ye keer for it."

She motioned shyly towards the cabin, and then led the way. The stranger, with an inarticulate murmur, afterwards disguised as a cough, followed her meekly. Nevertheless, by the time they had reached the cabin he had shaken his long hair over his eyes again, and a dark abstraction gathered chiefly in his eyebrows. But it did not efface from the girl's mind the previous concession of a blush, and, although it added to her curiosity, did not alarm her. He drank the milk awkwardly. But by the laws of courtesy, even among the most savage tribes, she felt he was, at that moment at least, harmless. A timid smile fluttered around her mouth as she said:—

"When ye hung up them things I thought ye might be havin' suthing to swap or sell. That is,"—with tactful politeness— "mother was wantin' a new skillet, and it would have been handy if you'd had one. But"—with an apologetic glance at his equipments—"if it ain't your business, it's all right, and no offense."

"I've got a lot o' skillets," said the strange teamster, with marked condescension, "and she can have one. They're all that's left outer a heap o' trader's stuff captured by Injuns t'other side of Laramie. We had a big fight to get 'em back. Lost two of our best men—scalped at Bloody Creek—and had to drop a dozen redskins in their tracks—me and another man—lyin' flat in er wagon and firin' under the flaps o' the canvas. I don't know ez they waz wuth it," he added in gloomy retrospect; "but I've got to get rid of 'em, I reckon, somehow, afore I work over to Deadman's Gulch again."

The young girl's eyes brightened timidly with a feminine mingling of imaginative awe and personal, pitying interest. He was, after all, so young and amiable looking for such hardships and adventures. And with all this, he—this Indian fighter—was a little afraid of HER!

"Then that's why you carry that knife and six-shooter?" she said. "But you won't want 'em now, here in the settlement."

"That's ez mebbe," said the stranger darkly. He paused, and then suddenly, as if recklessly accepting a dangerous risk, unbuckled his revolver and handed it abstractedly to the young girl. But the sheath of the bowie-knife was a fixture in his body-belt, and he was obliged to withdraw the glittering blade by itself, and to hand it to her in all its naked terrors. The young girl received the weapons with a smiling complacency. Upon such altars as these the skeptical reader will remember that Mars had once hung his "battered shield," his lance, and "uncontrolled crest."

Nevertheless, the warlike teamster was not without embarrassment. Muttering something about the necessity of "looking after his stock," he achieved a hesitating bow, backed awkwardly out of the door, and receiving from the conquering hands of the young girl his weapons again, was obliged to carry them somewhat ingloriously in his hands across the road, and put them on the wagon seat, where, in company with the culinary articles, they seemed to lose their distinctively aggressive character. Here, although his cheek was still flushed from his peaceful encounter, his voice regained some of its hoarse severity as he drove the oxen from the muddy pool into which they had luxuriantly wandered, and brought their fodder from the wagon. Later, as the sun was setting, he lit a corn-cob pipe, and somewhat ostentatiously strolled down the road, with a furtive eye lingering upon the still open door of the farmhouse. Presently two angular figures appeared from it, the farmer and his wife, intent on barter.

These he received with his previous gloomy preoccupation, and a slight variation of the story he had told their daughter. It is possible that his suggestive indifference piqued and heightened the bargaining instincts of the woman, for she not only bought the skillet, but purchased a clock and a roll of carpeting. Still more, in some effusion of rustic courtesy, she extended an invitation to him to sup with them, which he declined and accepted in the same embarrassed breath, returning the proffered hospitality by confidentially showing them a couple of dried scalps, presumably of Indian origin. It was in the same moment of human weakness that he answered their polite query as to "what they might call him," by intimating that his name was "Red Jim,"—a title of achievement by which he was generally known, which for the present must suffice them. But during the repast that followed this was shortened to "Mister Jim," and even familiarly by the elders to plain "Jim." Only the young girl habitually used the formal prefix in return for the "Miss Phoebe" that he called her.

With three such sympathetic and unexperienced auditors the gloomy embarrassment of Red Jim was soon dissipated, although it could hardly be said that he was generally communicative. Dark tales of Indian warfare, of night attacks and wild stampedes, in which he had always taken a prominent part, flowed freely from his lips, but little else of his past history or present prospects. And even his narratives of adventure were more or less fragmentary and imperfect in detail.

"You woz saying," said the farmer, with slow, matter of fact, New England deliberation, "ez how you guessed you woz beguiled amongst the Injins by your Mexican partner, a pow'ful influential man, and yet you woz the only one escaped the gen'ral slarterin'. How came the Injins to kill HIM—their friend?"

"They didn't," returned Jim, with ominously averted eyes.

"What became of him?" continued the farmer.

Red Jim shadowed his eyes with his hand, and cast a dark glance of scrutiny out of the doors and windows. The young girl perceived it with timid, fascinated concern, and said hurriedly:—

"Don't ask him, father! Don't you see he mustn't tell?"

"Not when spies may be hangin' round, and doggin' me at every step," said Red Jim, as if reflecting, with another furtive glance towards the already fading prospect without. "They've sworn to revenge him," he added moodily.

A momentary silence followed. The farmer coughed slightly, and looked dubiously at his wife. But the two women had already exchanged feminine glances of sympathy for this evident slayer of traitors, and were apparently inclined to stop any adverse criticism.

In the midst of which a shout was heard from the road. The

farmer and his family instinctively started. Red Jim alone remained unmoved—a fact which did not lessen the admiration of his feminine audience. The host rose quickly, and went out. The figure of a horseman had halted in the road, but after a few moments' conversation with the farmer they both moved towards the house and disappeared. When the farmer returned, it was to say that "one of them 'Frisco dandies, who didn't keer about stoppin' at the hotel in the settlement," had halted to give his "critter" a feed and drink that he might continue his journey. He had asked him to come in while the horse was feeding, but the stranger had "guessed he'd stretch his legs outside and smoke his cigar;" he might have thought the company "not fine enough for him," but he was "civil spoken enough, and had an all-fired smart hoss, and seemed to know how to run him." To the anxious inquiries of his wife and daughter he added that the stranger didn't seem like a spy or a Mexican; was "as young as HIM," pointing to the moody Red Jim, "and a darned sight more peaceful-like in style."

Perhaps owing to the criticism of the farmer, perhaps from some still lurking suspicion of being overheard by eaves-droppers, or possibly from a humane desire to relieve the strained apprehension of the women, Red Jim, as the farmer disappeared to rejoin the stranger, again dropped into a lighter and gentler vein of reminiscence. He told them how, when a mere boy, he had been lost from an emigrant train in company with a little girl some years his junior. How, when they found themselves alone on the desolate plain, with the vanished train beyond their reach, he endeavored to keep the child from a knowledge of the real danger of their position, and to soothe and comfort her. How he carried her on his back, until, exhausted, he sank in a heap of sage-brush. How he was surrounded by Indians, who, however, never suspected his hiding-place; and how he remained motionless and breathless with the sleeping child for three hours, until they departed. How, at the last moment, he had perceived a train in the distance, and had staggered with her thither, although shot at and wounded by the trainmen in the belief that he was an Indian. How it was afterwards discovered that the child was the long-lost daughter of a millionaire; how he had resolutely refused any gratuity for saving her, and she was now a peerless young heiress, famous in California. Whether this lighter tone of narrative suited him better, or whether the active feminine sympathy of his auditors helped him along, certain it was that his story was more coherent and intelligible and his voice less hoarse and constrained than in his previous belligerent reminiscences; his expression changed, and even his features worked into something like gentler emotion. The bright eyes of Phoebe, fastened upon him, turned dim with a faint moisture, and her pale cheek took upon itself a little color. The mother, after interjecting "Du tell," and "I wanter know," remained open-mouthed, staring at her visitor. And in the silence that followed, a pleasant, but somewhat melancholy voice came from the open door.

"I beg your pardon, but I thought I couldn't be mistaken. It IS my old friend, Jim Hooker!"

Everybody started. Red Jim stumbled to his feet with an inarticulate and hysteric exclamation. Yet the apparition that now stood in the doorway was far from being terrifying or discomposing. It was evidently the stranger—a slender, elegantly-knit figure, whose upper lip was faintly shadowed by a soft, dark mustache indicating early manhood, and whose unstudied ease in his well-fitting garments bespoke the dweller of cities. Good-looking and well-dressed, without the consciousness of being either; self-possessed through easy circumstances, yet without self-assertion; courteous by nature and instinct as well as from an experience of granting favors, he might have been a welcome addition to even a more critical company. But Red Jim, hurriedly seizing his outstretched hand, instantly dragged him away from the doorway into the road and out of hearing of his audience.

"Did you hear what I was saying?" he asked hoarsely.

"Well, yes—I think so," returned the stranger, with a quiet smile.

"Ye ain't goin' back on me, Clarence, are ye—ain't goin' to gimme away afore them, old pard, are ye?" said Jim, with a sudden change to almost pathetic pleading.

"No," returned the stranger, smiling. "And certainly not before that interested young lady, Jim. But stop. Let me look at you."

He held out both hands, took Jim's, spread them apart for a moment with a boyish gesture, and, looking in his face, said half mischievously, half sadly, "Yes, it's the same old Jim Hooker—unchanged."

"But YOU'RE changed—reg'lar war paint, Big Injin style!" said Hooker, looking up at him with an awkward mingling of admiration and envy. "Heard you struck it rich with the old man, and was Mister Brant now!"

"Yes," said Clarence gently, yet with a smile that had not only a tinge of weariness but even of sadness in it.

Unfortunately, the act, which was quite natural to Clarence's sensitiveness, and indeed partly sprang from some concern in his old companion's fortunes, translated itself by a very human process to Hooker's consciousness as a piece of rank affectation. HE would have been exalted and exultant in Clarence's place, consequently any other exhibition was only "airs." Nevertheless, at the present moment Clarence was to be placated.

"You didn't mind my telling that story about your savin' Susy as my own, did ye?" he said, with a hasty glance over his shoulder. "I only did it to fool the old man and women-folks, and make talk. You won't blow on me? Ye ain't mad about it?"

It had crossed Clarence's memory that when they were both younger Jim Hooker had once not only borrowed his story, but his name and personality as well. Yet in his loyalty to old memories there was mingled no resentment for past injury. "Of course not," he said, with a smile that was, however, still thoughtful. "Why should I? Only I ought to tell you that Susy Peyton is living with her adopted parents not ten miles from here, and it might reach their ears. She's quite a young lady now, and if I wouldn't tell her story to strangers, I don't think YOU ought to, Jim."

He said this so pleasantly that even the skeptical Jim forgot what he believed were the "airs and graces" of self-abnegation, and said, "Let's go inside, and I'll introduce you," and turned to the house. But Clarence Brant drew back. "I'm going on as soon as my horse is fed, for I'm on a visit to Peyton, and I intend to push as far as Santa Inez still to-night. I want to talk with you about yourself, Jim," he added gently; "your prospects and your future. I heard," he went on hesitatingly, "that you were—at work—in a restaurant in San Francisco. I'm glad to see that you are at least your own master here,"—he glanced at the wagon. "You are selling things, I suppose? For yourself, or another? Is that team yours? Come," he added, still pleasantly, but in an older and graver voice, with perhaps the least touch of experienced authority, "be frank, Jim. Which is it? Never mind what things you've told IN THERE, tell ME the truth about yourself. Can I help you in any way? Believe me, I should like to. We have been old friends, whatever difference in our luck, I am yours still."

Thus adjured, the redoubtable Jim, in a hoarse whisper, with a furtive eye on the house, admitted that he was traveling for an itinerant peddler, whom he expected to join later in the settlement; that he had his own methods of disposing of his wares, and (darkly) that his proprietor and the world generally had better not interfere with him; that (with a return to more confidential lightness) he had already "worked the Wild West Injin" business so successfully as to dispose of his wares, particularly in yonder house, and might do even more if not prematurely and wantonly "blown upon," "gone back on," or "given away."

"But wouldn't you like to settle down on some bit of land like this, and improve it for yourself?" said Clarence. "All these valley terraces are bound to rise in value, and meantime you would be independent. It could be managed, Jim. I think I could arrange it for you," he went on, with a slight glow of youthful enthusiasm. "Write to me at Peyton's ranch, and I'll see you when I come back, and we'll hunt up something for you together." As Jim received the proposition with a kind of gloomy embarrassment, he added lightly, with a glance at the farmhouse, "It might be near HERE, you know; and you'd have pleasant neighbors, and even eager listeners to your old adventures."

"You'd better come in a minit before you go," said Jim, clumsily evading a direct reply. Clarence hesitated a moment, and then yielded. For an equal moment Jim Hooker was torn between secret jealousy of his old comrade's graces and a desire to present them as familiar associations of his own. But his vanity was quickly appeased.

Need it be said that the two women received this fleck and foam of a super-civilization they knew little of as almost an impertinence compared to the rugged, gloomy, pathetic, and equally youthful hero of an adventurous wilderness of which they knew still less? What availed the courtesy and gentle melancholy of Clarence Brant beside the mysterious gloom and dark savagery of Red Jim? Yet they received him patronizingly, as one who was, like themselves, an admirer of manly grace and power, and the recipient of Jim's friendship. The farmer alone seemed to prefer Clarence, and yet the latter's tacit indorsement of Red Jim, through his evident previous intimacy with him, impressed the man in Jim's favor. All of which Clarence saw with that sensitive perception which had given him an early insight into human weakness, yet still had never shaken his youthful optimism. He smiled a little thoughtfully, but was openly fraternal to Jim, courteous to his host and family, and, as he rode away in the faint moonlight, magnificently opulent in his largess to the farmer—his first and only assertion of his position.

The farmhouse, straggling barn, and fringe of dusty willows, the white dome of the motionless wagon, with the hanging frying pans and kettles showing in the moonlight like black silhouettes against the staring canvas, all presently sank behind Clarence like the details of a dream, and he was alone with the moon, the hazy mystery of the level, grassy plain, and the monotony of the unending road. As he rode slowly along he thought of that other dreary plain, white with alkali patches and brown with rings of deserted camp-fires, known to his boyhood of deprivation, dependency, danger, and adventure, oddly enough, with a strange delight; and his later years of study, monastic seclusion, and final ease and independence, with an easy sense of wasted existence and useless waiting. He remembered his homeless childhood in the South, where servants and slaves took the place of the father he had never known, and the mother that he rarely saw; he remembered his abandonment to a mysterious female relation, where his natural guardians seemed to have overlooked and forgotten him, until he was sent, an all too young adventurer, to work his passage on an overland emigrant train across the plains; he remembered, as yesterday, the fears, the hopes, the dreams and dangers of that momentous journey. He recalled his little playmate, Susy, and their strange adventures—the whole incident that the imaginative Jim Hooker had translated and rehearsed as his own—rose vividly before him. He thought of the cruel end of that pilgrimage, which again left him homeless and forgotten by even the relative he was seeking in a strange land. He remembered his solitary journey to the gold mines, taken with a boy's trust and a boy's fearlessness, and the strange protector he had found there, who had news of his missing kinsman; he remembered how this protector—whom he had at once instinctively loved—transferred him to the house of this new-found relation, who treated him kindly and sent him to the Jesuit school, but who never awakened in him a feeling of kinship. He dreamed again of his life at school, his accidental meeting with Susy at Santa Clara, the keen revival of his boyish love for his old playmate, now a pretty schoolgirl, the petted adopted child of wealthy parents. He recalled the terrible shock that interrupted this boyish episode: the news of the death of his protector, and the revelation that this hard, silent, and mysterious man was his own father, whose reckless life and desperate reputation had impelled him to assume a disguise.

He remembered how his sudden accession to wealth and independence had half frightened him, and had always left a lurking sensitiveness that he was unfairly favored, by some mere accident, above his less lucky companions. The rude vices of his old associates had made him impatient of the feebler sensual indulgences of the later companions of his luxury, and exposed their hollow fascinations; his sensitive fastidiousness kept him clean among vulgar temptations; his clear perceptions were never blinded by selfish sophistry. Meantime his feeling for Susy remained unchanged. Pride had kept him from seeking the Peytons. His present visit was as unpremeditated as Peyton's invitation had been unlooked for by him. Yet he had not allowed himself to be deceived. He knew that this courtesy was probably due to the change in his fortune, although he had hoped it might have been some change in their opinion brought about by Susy. But he would at least see her again, not in the pretty, half-clandestine way she had thought necessary, but openly and as her equal.

In his rapid ride he seemed to have suddenly penetrated the peaceful calm of the night. The restless irritation of the afternoon trade winds had subsided; the tender moonlight had hushed and tranquilly possessed the worried plain; the unending files of wild oats, far spaced and distinct, stood erect and motionless as trees; something of the sedate solemnity of a great forest seemed to have fallen upon their giant stalks. There was no dew. In that light, dry air, the heavier dust no longer rose beneath the heels of his horse, whose flying shadow passed over the field like a cloud, leaving no trail or track behind it. In the preoccupation of his thought and his breathless retrospect, the young man had ridden faster than he intended, and he now checked his panting horse. The influence of the night and the hushed landscape stole over him; his thoughts took a gentler turn; in that dim, mysterious horizon line before him, his future seemed to be dreamily peopled with airy, graceful shapes that more or less took the likeness of Susy. She was bright, coquettish, romantic, as he had last seen her; she was older, graver, and thoughtfully welcome of him; or she was cold, distant, and severely forgetful of the past. How would her adopted father and mother receive him? Would they ever look upon him in the light of a suitor to the young girl? He had no fear of Peyton—he understood his own sex, and, young as he was, knew already how to make himself respected; but how could he overcome that instinctive aversion which Mrs. Peyton had so often made him feel he had provoked? Yet in this dreamy hush of earth and sky, what was not possible? His boyish heart beat high with daring visions.

He saw Mrs. Peyton in the porch, welcoming him with that maternal smile which his childish longing had so often craved to share with Susy. Peyton would be there, too— Peyton, who had once pushed back his torn straw hat to look approvingly in his boyish eyes; and Peyton, perhaps, might be proud of him.

Suddenly he started. A voice in his very ear!

"Bah! A yoke of vulgar cattle grazing on lands that were thine by right and law. Neither more nor less than that. And I tell thee, Pancho, like cattle, to be driven off or caught and branded for one's own. Ha! There are those who could swear to the truth of this on the Creed. Ay! and bring papers stamped and signed by the governor's rubric to prove it. And not that I hate them—bah! what are those heretic swine to me? But thou dost comprehend me? It galls and pricks me to see them swelling themselves with stolen husks, and men like thee, Pancho, ousted from their own land."

Clarence had halted in utter bewilderment. No one was visible before him, behind him, on either side. The words, in Spanish, came from the air, the sky, the distant horizon, he knew not which. Was he still dreaming? A strange shiver crept over his skin as if the air had grown suddenly chill. Then another mysterious voice arose, incredulous, half mocking, but equally distinct and clear.

"Caramba! What is this? You are wandering, friend Pancho.

You are still smarting from his tongue. He has the grant confirmed by his brigand government; he has the POSSESSION, stolen by a thief like himself; and he has the Corregidors with him. For is he not one of them himself, this Judge Peyton?"

Peyton! Clarence felt the blood rush back to his face in astonishment and indignation. His heels mechanically pressed his horse's flanks, and the animal sprang forward.

"Guarda! Mira!" said the voice again in a quicker, lower tone. But this time it was evidently in the field beside him, and the heads and shoulders of two horsemen emerged at the same moment from the tall ranks of wild oats. The mystery was solved. The strangers had been making their way along a lower level of the terraced plain, hidden by the grain, not twenty yards away, and parallel with the road they were now ascending to join. Their figures were alike formless in long striped serapes, and their features undistinguishable under stiff black sombreros.

"Buenas noches, senor," said the second voice, in formal and cautious deliberation.

A sudden inspiration made Clarence respond in English, as if he had not comprehended the stranger's words, "Eh?"

"Gooda-nighta," repeated the stranger.

"Oh, good-night," returned Clarence. They passed him. Their spurs tinkled twice or thrice, their mustangs sprang forward, and the next moment the loose folds of their serapes were fluttering at their sides like wings in their flight.

CHAPTER IV

After the chill of a dewless night the morning sun was apt to look ardently upon the Robles Rancho, if so strong an expression could describe the dry, oven-like heat of a Californian coast-range valley. Before ten o'clock the adobe wall of the patio was warm enough to permit lingering vacqueros and idle peons to lean against it, and the exposed annexe was filled with sharp, resinous odors from the oozing sap of unseasoned "redwood" boards, warped and drying in the hot sunshine. Even at that early hour the climbing Castilian roses were drooping against the wooden columns of the new veranda, scarcely older than themselves, and mingling an already faded spice with the aroma of baking wood and the more material fragrance of steaming coffee, that seemed dominant everywhere.

In fact, the pretty breakfast-room, whose three broad windows, always open to the veranda, gave an al fresco effect to every meal, was a pathetic endeavor of the Southern-bred Peyton to emulate the soft, luxurious, and open-air indolence of his native South, in a climate that was not only not tropical, but even austere in its most fervid moments. Yet, although cold draughts invaded it from the rear that morning, Judge Peyton sat alone, between the open doors and windows, awaiting the slow coming of his wife and the young ladies. He was not in an entirely comfortable mood that morning. Things were not going on well at Robles. That truculent vagabond, Pedro, had, the night before, taken himself off with a curse that had frightened even the vacqueros, who most hated him as a companion, but who now seemed inclined to regard his absence as an injury done to their race. Peyton, uneasily conscious that his own anger had been excited by an exaggerated conception of the accident, was now, like most obstinate men, inclined to exaggerate the importance of Pedro's insolence. He was well out of it to get rid of this quarrelsome hanger-on, whose presumption and ill-humor threatened the discipline of the rancho, yet he could not entirely forget that he had employed him on account of his family claims, and from a desire to placate racial jealousy and settle local differences. For the inferior Mexicans and Indian half-breeds still regarded their old masters with affection; were, in fact, more concerned for the integrity of their caste than the masters were themselves, and the old Spanish families who had made alliances with Americans, and shared their land with them, had rarely succeeded in alienating their retainers with their lands. Certain experiences in the proving of his grant before the Land Commission had taught Peyton that they were not to be depended upon. And lately there had been unpleasant rumors of the discovery of some unlooked-for claimants to a division of the grant itself, which might affect his own title.

He looked up quickly as voices and light steps on the veranda at last heralded the approach of his tardy household from the corridor. But, in spite of his preoccupation, he was startled and even awkwardly impressed with a change in Susy's appearance. She was wearing, for the first time, a long skirt, and this sudden maturing of her figure struck him, as a man, much more forcibly than it would probably have impressed a woman, more familiar with details. He had not noticed certain indications of womanhood, as significant, perhaps, in her carriage as her outlines, which had been lately perfectly apparent to her mother and Mary, but which were to him now, for the first time, indicated by a few inches of skirt. She not only looked taller to his masculine eyes, but these few inches had added to the mystery as well as the drapery of the goddess; they were not so much the revelation of maturity as the suggestion that it was HIDDEN. So impressed was he, that a half-serious lecture on her yesterday's childishness, the outcome of his irritated reflections that morning, died upon his lips. He felt he was no longer dealing with a child.

He welcomed them with that smile of bantering approbation, supposed to keep down inordinate vanity, which for some occult reason one always reserves for the members of one's own family. He was quite conscious that Susy was looking very pretty in this new and mature frock, and that as she stood beside his wife, far from ageing Mrs. Peyton's good looks and figure, she appeared like an equal companion, and that they mutually "became" one another. This, and the fact that they were all, including Mary Rogers, in their freshest, gayest morning dresses, awakened a half-humorous, half-real apprehension in his mind, that he was now hopelessly surrounded by a matured sex, and in a weak minority.

"I think I ought to have been prepared," he began grimly, "for this addition to—to—the skirts of my family."

"Why, John," returned Mrs. Peyton quickly; "do you mean to say you haven't noticed that the poor child has for weeks been looking positively indecent?"

"Really, papa, I've been a sight to behold. Haven't I, Mary?" chimed in Susy.

"Yes, dear. Why, Judge, I've been wondering that Susy stood it so well, and never complained."

Peyton glanced around him at this compact feminine embattlement. It was as he feared. Yet even here he was again at fault.

"And," said Mrs. Peyton slowly, with the reserved significance of the feminine postscript in her voice, "if that Mr. Brant is coming here to-day, it would be just as well for him to see that SHE IS NO LONGER A CHILD, AS WHEN HE KNEW HER."

An hour later, good-natured Mary Rogers, in her character of "a dear,"—which was usually indicated by the undertaking of small errands for her friend—was gathering roses from the old garden for Susy's adornment, when she saw a vision which lingered with her for many a day. She had stopped to look through the iron grille in the adobe wall, across the open wind-swept plain. Miniature waves were passing over the wild oats, with glittering disturbances here and there in the depressions like the sparkling of green foam; the horizon line was sharply defined against the hard, steel-blue sky; everywhere the brand-new morning was shining with almost painted brilliancy; the vigor, spirit, and even crudeness of youth were over all. The young girl was dazzled and bewildered. Suddenly, as if blown out of the waving grain, or an incarnation of the vivid morning, the bright and striking figure of a youthful horseman flashed before the grille. It was Clarence Brant! Mary Rogers had always seen him, in the loyalty of friendship, with Susy's prepossessed eyes, yet she fancied that morning that he had never looked so handsome before. Even the foppish fripperies of his riding-dress and silver trappings seemed as much the natural expression of conquering youth as the invincible morning sunshine. Perhaps it might have been a reaction against Susy's caprice or some latent susceptibility of her own; but a momentary antagonism to her friend stirred even her kindly nature. What right had Susy to trifle with such an opportunity? Who was SHE to hesitate over this gallant prince?

But Prince Charming's quick eyes had detected her, and the next moment his beautiful horse was beside the grating, and his ready hand of greeting extended through the bars.

"I suppose I am early and unexpected, but I slept at Santa Inez last night, that I might ride over in the cool of the morning. My things are coming by the stage-coach, later. It seemed such a slow way of coming one's self."

Mary Rogers's black eyes intimated that the way he had taken was the right one, but she gallantly recovered herself and remembered her position as confidante. And here was the opportunity of delivering Susy's warning unobserved. She withdrew her hand from Clarence's frank grasp, and passing it through the grating, patted the sleek, shining flanks of his horse, with a discreet division of admiration.

"And such a lovely creature, too! And Susy will be so delighted! and oh, Mr. Brant, please, you're to say nothing of having met her at Santa Clara. It's just as well not to begin with THAT here, for, you see" (with a large, maternal manner), "you were both SO young then."

Clarence drew a quick breath. It was the first check to his vision of independence and equal footing! Then his invitation was NOT the outcome of a continuous friendship revived by Susy, as he had hoped; the Peytons had known nothing of his meeting with her, or perhaps they would not have invited him. He was here as an impostor—and all because Susy had chosen to make a mystery of a harmless encounter, which might have been explained, and which they might have even countenanced. He thought bitterly of his old playmate for a brief moment—as brief as Mary's antagonism.

The young girl noticed the change in his face, but misinterpreted it.

"Oh, there's no danger of its coming out if you don't say anything," she said, quickly. "Ride on to the house, and don't wait for me. You'll find them in the patio on the veranda."

Clarence moved on, but not as spiritedly as before. Nevertheless there was still dash enough about him and the animal he bestrode to stir into admiration the few lounging vacqueros of a country which was apt to judge the status of a rider by the quality of his horse. Nor was the favorable impression confined to them alone. Peyton's gratification rang out cheerily in his greeting:—

"Bravo, Clarence! You are here in true caballero style. Thanks for the compliment to the rancho."

For a moment the young man was transported back again to his boyhood, and once more felt Peyton's approving hand pushing back the worn straw hat from his childish forehead. A faint color rose to his cheeks; his eyes momentarily dropped. The highest art could have done no more! The slight aggressiveness of his youthful finery and picturesque good looks was condoned at once; his modesty conquered where self-assertion might have provoked opposition, and even Mrs. Peyton felt herself impelled to come forward with an outstretched hand scarcely less frank than her husband's. Then Clarence lifted his eyes. He saw before him the woman to whom his childish heart had gone out with the inscrutable longing and adoration of a motherless, homeless, comp-anionless boy; the woman who had absorbed the love of his playmate without sharing it with him; who had showered her protecting and maternal caresses on Susy, a waif like himself, yet had not only left his heart lonely and desolate, but had even added to his childish distrust of himself the thought that he had excited her aversion. He saw her more beautiful than ever in her restored health, freshness of coloring, and mature roundness of outline. He was unconsciously touched with a man's admiration for her without losing his boyish yearnings and half-filial affection; in her new materialistic womanhood his youthful imagination had lifted her to a queen and goddess. There was all this appeal in his still boyish eyes—eyes that had never yet known shame or fear in the expression of their emotions; there was all this in the gesture with which he lifted Mrs. Peyton's fingers to his lips. The little group saw in this act only a Spanish courtesy in keeping with his accepted role. But a thrill of surprise, of embarrassment, of intense gratification passed over her. For he had not even looked at Susy!

Her relenting was graceful. She welcomed him with a winning smile. Then she motioned pleasantly towards Susy.

"But here is an older friend, Mr. Brant, whom you do not seem to recognize—Susy, whom you have not seen since she was a child."

A quick flush rose to Clarence's cheek. The group smiled at this evident youthful confession of some boyish admiration. But Clarence knew that his truthful blood was merely resenting the deceit his lips were sealed from divulging. He did not dare to glance at Susy; it added to the general amusement that the young girl was obliged to present herself. But in this interval she had exchanged glances with Mary Rogers, who had rejoined the group, and she knew she was safe. She smiled with gracious condescension at Clarence; observed, with the patronizing superiority of age and established position, that he had GROWN, but had not greatly changed, and, it is needless to say, again filled her mother's heart with joy. Clarence, still intoxicated with Mrs. Peyton's kindliness, and, perhaps, still embarrassed by remorse, had not time to remark the girl's studied attitude. He shook hands with her cordially, and then, in the quick reaction of youth, accepted with humorous gravity the elaborate introduction to Mary Rogers by Susy, which completed this little comedy. And if, with a woman's quickness, Mrs. Peyton detected a certain lingering glance which passed between Mary Rogers and Clarence, and misinterpreted it, it was only a part of that mystification into which these youthful actors are apt to throw their mature audiences.

"Confess, Ally," said Peyton, cheerfully, as the three young people suddenly found their tongues with aimless vivacity and inconsequent laughter, and started with unintelligible spirits for an exploration of the garden, "confess now that your bete noir is really a very manly as well as a very presentable young fellow. By Jove! the padres have made a Spanish swell out of him without spoiling the Brant grit, either! Come, now; you're not afraid that Susy's style will suffer from HIS companionship. 'Pon my soul, she might borrow a little of his courtesy to his elders without indelicacy. I only wish she had as sincere a way of showing her respect for you as he has. Did you notice that he really didn't seem to see anybody else but you at first? And yet you never were a friend to him, like Susy."

The lady tossed her head slightly, but smiled.

"This is the first time he's seen Mary Rogers, isn't it?" she said meditatively.

"I reckon. But what's that to do with his politeness to you?"

"And do her parents know him?" she continued, without replying.

"How do I know? I suppose everybody has heard of him. Why?"

"Because I think they've taken a fancy to each other."

"What in the name of folly, Ally"—began the despairing Peyton.

"When you invite a handsome, rich, and fascinating young man into the company of young ladies, John," returned Mrs. Peyton, in her severest manner, "you must not forget you owe a certain responsibility to the parents. I shall certainly look after Miss Rogers."

CHAPTER V

Although the three young people had left the veranda together, when they reached the old garden Clarence and Susy found themselves considerably in advance of Mary Rogers, who had become suddenly and deeply interested in the beauty of a passion vine near the gate. At the first discovery of their isolation their voluble exchange of information about themselves and their occupations since their last meeting stopped simultaneously. Clarence, who had forgotten his momentary irritation, and had recovered his old happiness in her presence, was nevertheless conscious of some other change in her than that suggested by the lengthened skirt and the later and more delicate accentuation of her prettiness. It was not her affectation of superiority and older social experience, for that was only the outcome of what he had found charming in her as a child, and which he still good-humoredly accepted; nor was it her characteristic exaggeration of speech, which he still pleasantly recognized. It was something else, vague and indefinite—something that had been unnoticed while Mary was with them, but had now come between them like some unknown presence which had taken the confidante's place. He remained silent, looking at her half-brightening cheek and conscious profile. Then he spoke with awkward directness.

"You are changed, Susy, more than in looks."

"Hush," said the girl in a tragic whisper, with a warning gesture towards the blandly unconscious Mary.

"But," returned Clarence wonderingly, "she's your—our friend, you know."

"I DON'T know," said Susy, in a still deeper tone, "that is—oh, don't ask me! But when you're always surrounded by spies, when you can't say your soul is your own, you doubt everybody!" There was such a pretty distress in her violet eyes and curving eyebrows, that Clarence, albeit vague as to its origin and particulars, nevertheless possessed himself of the little hand that was gesticulating dangerously near his own, and pressed it sympathetically. Perhaps preoccupied with her emotions, she did not immediately withdraw it, as she went on rapidly: "And if you were cooped up here, day after day, behind these bars," pointing to the grille, "you'd know what I suffer."

"But"—began Clarence.

"Hush!" said Susy, with a stamp of her little foot.

Clarence, who had only wished to point out that the whole lower end of the garden wall was in ruins and the grille really was no prevention, "hushed."

"And listen! Don't pay me much attention to-day, but talk to HER," indicating the still discreet and distant Mary, "before father and mother. Not a word to her of this confidence, Clarence. To-morrow ride out alone on your beautiful horse, and come back by way of the woods, beyond our turning, at four o'clock. There's a trail to the right of the big madrono tree. Take that. Be careful and keep a good lookout, for she mustn't see you."

"Who mustn't see me?" said the puzzled Clarence.

"Why, Mary, of course, you silly boy!" returned the girl impatiently. "She'll be looking for ME. Go now, Clarence! Stop! Look at that lovely big maiden's-blush up there," pointing to a pink-suffused specimen of rose grandiflora hanging on the wall. "Get it, Clarence—that one—I'll show you where—there!" They had already plunged into the leafy bramble, and, standing on tiptoe, with her hand on his shoulder and head upturned, Susy's cheek had innocently approached Clarence's own. At this moment Clarence, possibly through some confusion of color, fragrance, or softness of contact, seemed to have availed himself of the opportunity, in a way which caused Susy to instantly rejoin Mary Rogers with affected dignity, leaving him to follow a few moments later with the captured flower.

Without trying to understand the reason of to-morrow's rendezvous, and perhaps not altogether convinced of the reality of Susy's troubles, he, however, did not find that difficulty in carrying out her other commands which he had expected. Mrs. Peyton was still gracious, and, with feminine tact, induced him to talk of himself, until she was presently in possession of his whole history, barring the episode of his meeting with Susy, since he had parted with them. He felt a strange satisfaction in familiarly pouring out his confidences to this superior woman, whom he had always held in awe. There was a new delight in her womanly interest in his trials and adventures, and a subtle pleasure even in her half-motherly criticism and admonition of some passages. I am afraid he forgot Susy, who listened with the complacency of an exhibitor; Mary, whose black eyes dilated alternately with sympathy for the performer and deprecation of Mrs. Peyton's critical glances; and Peyton, who, however, seemed lost in thought, and preoccupied. Clarence was happy. The softly shaded lights in the broad, spacious, comfortably furnished drawing-room shone on the group before him. It was a picture of refined domesticity which the homeless Clarence had never known except as a vague, half-painful, boyish remembrance; it was a realization of welcome that far exceeded his wildest boyish vision of the preceding night. With that recollection came another—a more uneasy one. He remembered how that vision had been interrupted by the strange voices in the road, and their vague but ominous import to his host. A feeling of self-reproach came over him. The threats had impressed him as only mere braggadocio— he knew the characteristic exaggeration of the race—but perhaps he ought to privately tell Peyton of the incident at once.

The opportunity came later, when the ladies had retired, and Peyton, wrapped in a poncho in a rocking-chair, on the now chilly veranda, looked up from his reverie and a cigar. Clarence casually introduced the incident, as if only for the sake of describing the supernatural effect of the hidden voices, but he was concerned to see that Peyton was considerably disturbed by their more material import. After questioning him as to the appearance of the two men, his host said: "I don't mind telling you, Clarence, that as far as that fellow's intentions go he is quite sincere, although his threats are only borrowed thunder. He is a man whom I have just dismissed for carelessness and insolence—two things that run in double harness in this country—but I should be more afraid to find him at my back on a dark night, alone on the plains; than to confront him in daylight, in the witness box, against me. He was only repeating a silly rumor that the title to this rancho and the nine square leagues beyond would be attacked by some speculators."

"But I thought your title was confirmed two years ago," said Clarence.

"The GRANT was confirmed," returned Peyton, "which means that the conveyance of the Mexican government of these lands to the ancestor of Victor Robles was held to be legally proven by the United States Land Commission, and a patent issued to all those who held under it. I and my neighbors hold under it by purchase from Victor Robles, subject to the confirmation of the Land Commission. But that confirmation was only of Victor's GREAT-GRANDFATHER'S TITLE, and it is now alleged that as Victor's father died without making a will, Victor has claimed and disposed of property which he ought to have divided with his SISTERS. At least, some speculating rascals in San Francisco have set up what they call 'the Sisters' title,' and are selling it to actual settlers on the unoccupied lands beyond. As, by the law, it would hold possession against the mere ordinary squatters, whose only right is based, as you know, on the presumption that there is NO TITLE CLAIMED, it gives the possessor immunity to enjoy the use of the property until the case is decided, and even should the original title hold good against his, the successful litigant would probably be willing to pay for improvements and possession to save the expensive and tedious process of ejectment."

"But this does not affect YOU, who have already possession?" said Clarence quickly.

"No, not as far as THIS HOUSE and the lands I actually OCCUPY AND CULTIVATE are concerned; and they know that I am safe to fight to the last, and carry the case to the Supreme Court in that case, until the swindle is exposed, or they drop it; but I may have to pay them something to keep the squatters off my UNOCCUPIED land."

"But you surely wouldn't recognize those rascals in any way?" said the astonished Clarence.

"As against other rascals? Why not?" returned Peyton grimly. "I only pay for the possession which their sham title gives me to my own land. If by accident that title obtains, I am still on the safe side." After a pause he said, more gravely, "What you overheard, Clarence, shows me that the plan is more forward than I had imagined, and that I may have to fight traitors here."

"I hope, sir," said Clarence, with a quick glow in his earnest face, "that you'll let me help you. You thought I did once, you remember—with the Indians."

There was so much of the old Clarence in his boyish appeal and eager, questioning face that Peyton, who had been talking to him as a younger but equal man of affairs, was startled into a smile, "You did, Clarence, though the Indians butchered your friends, after all. I don't know, though, but that your experiences with those Spaniards—you must have known a lot of them when you were with Don Juan Robinson and at the college—might be of service in getting at evidence, or smashing their witnesses if it comes to a fight. But just now, MONEY is everything. They must be bought OFF THE LAND if I have to mortgage it for the purpose. That strikes you as a rather heroic remedy, Clarence, eh?" he continued, in his old, half-bantering attitude towards Clarence's inexperienced youth, "don't it?"

But Clarence was not thinking of that. Another more audacious but equally youthful and enthusiastic idea had taken possession of his mind, and he lay awake half that night revolving it. It was true that it was somewhat imprac-tically mixed with his visions of Mrs. Peyton and Susy, and even included his previous scheme of relief for the improvident and incorrigible Hooker. But it gave a wonderful sincerity and happiness to his slumbers that night, which the wiser and elder Peyton might have envied, and I wot not was in the long run as correct and sagacious as Peyton's sleepless cogitations. And in the early morning Mr. Clarence Brant, the young capitalist, sat down to his traveling-desk and wrote two clear-headed, logical, and practical business letters—one to his banker, and the other to his former guardian, Don Juan Robinson, as his first step in a resolve that was, nevertheless, perhaps as wildly quixotic and enthusiastic as any dream his boyish and unselfish heart had ever indulged.

At breakfast, in the charmed freedom of the domestic circle, Clarence forgot Susy's capricious commands of yesterday, and began to address himself to her in his old earnest fashion, until he was warned by a significant knitting of the young lady's brows and monosyllabic responses. But in his youthful loyalty to Mrs. Peyton, he was more pained to notice Susy's occasional unconscious indifference to her adopted mother's affectionate expression, and a more conscious disregard of her wishes. So uneasy did he become, in his sensitive concern for Mrs. Peyton's half-concealed mortification, that he gladly accepted Peyton's offer to go with him to visit the farm and corral. As the afternoon approached, with another twinge of self-reproach, he was obliged to invent some excuse to decline certain hospitable plans of Mrs. Peyton's for his entertainment, and at half past three stole somewhat guiltily, with his horse, from the stables. But he had to pass before the outer wall of the garden and grille, through which he had seen Mary the day before. Raising his eyes mechanically, he was startled to see Mrs. Peyton standing behind the grating, with her abstracted gaze fixed upon the wind-tossed, level grain beyond her. She smiled as she saw him, but there were traces of tears in her proud, handsome eyes.

"You are going to ride?" she said pleasantly.

"Y-e-es," stammered the shamefaced Clarence.

She glanced at him wistfully.

"You are right. The girls have gone away by themselves. Mr. Peyton has ridden over to Santa Inez on this dreadful land business, and I suppose you'd have found him a dull riding companion. It is rather stupid here. I quite envy you, Mr. Brant, your horse and your freedom."

"But, Mrs. Peyton," broke in Clarence, impulsively, "you have a horse—I saw it, a lovely lady's horse—eating its head off in the stable. Won't you let me run back and order it; and won't you, please, come out with me for a good, long gallop?"

He meant what he said. He had spoken quickly, impulsively, but with the perfect understanding in his own mind that his proposition meant the complete abandonment of his rendezvous with Susy. Mrs. Peyton was astounded and slightly stirred with his earnestness, albeit unaware of all it implied.

"It's a great temptation, Mr. Brant," she said, with a playful smile, which dazzled Clarence with its first faint suggestion of a refined woman's coquetry; "but I'm afraid that Mr. Peyton would think me going mad in my old age. No. Go on and enjoy your gallop, and if you should see those giddy girls anywhere, send them home early for chocolate, before the cold wind gets up."

She turned, waved her slim white hand playfully in acknowledgment of Clarence's bared head, and moved away.

For the first few moments the young man tried to find relief in furious riding, and in bullying his spirited horse. Then he

60   Bret Harte

pulled quickly up. What was he doing? What was he going to do? What foolish, vapid deceit was this that he was going to practice upon that noble, queenly, confiding, generous woman? (He had already forgotten that she had always distrusted him.) What a fool he was not to tell her half-jokingly that he expected to meet Susy! But would he have dared to talk half-jokingly to such a woman on such a topic? And would it have been honorable without disclosing the WHOLE truth—that they had met secretly before? And was it fair to Susy?—dear, innocent, childish Susy! Yet something must be done! It was such trivial, purposeless deceit, after all; for this noble woman, Mrs. Peyton, so kind, so gentle, would never object to his loving Susy and marrying her. And they would all live happily together; and Mrs. Peyton would never be separated from them, but always beaming tenderly upon them as she did just now in the garden. Yes, he would have a serious understanding with Susy, and that would excuse the clandestine meeting to-day.

His rapid pace, meantime, had brought him to the imperceptible incline of the terrace, and he was astonished, in turning in the saddle, to find that the casa, corral, and outbuildings had completely vanished, and that behind him rolled only the long sea of grain, which seemed to have swallowed them in its yellowing depths. Before him lay the wooded ravine through which the stagecoach passed, which was also the entrance to the rancho, and there, too, probably, was the turning of which Susy had spoken. But it was still early for the rendezvous; indeed, he was in no hurry to meet her in his present discontented state, and he made a listless circuit of the field, in the hope of discovering the phenomena that had caused the rancho's mysterious disappearance. When he had found that it was the effect of the different levels, his attention was arrested by a multitude of moving objects in a still more distant field, which proved to be a band of wild horses. In and out among them, circling aimlessly, as it seemed to him, appeared two horsemen apparently performing some mystic evolution. To add to their singular performance, from time to time one of the flying herd, driven by the horsemen far beyond the circle of its companions, dropped suddenly and unaccountably in full career. The field closed over it as if it had been swallowed up. In a few moments it appeared again, trotting peacefully behind its former pursuer. It was some time before Clarence grasped the meaning of this strange spectacle. Although the clear, dry atmosphere sharply accented the silhouette-like outlines of the men and horses, so great was the distance that the slender forty-foot lasso, which in the skillful hands of the horsemen had effected these captures, was COMPLETELY INVISIBLE! The horsemen were Peyton's vacqueros, making a selection from the young horses for the market. He remembered now that Peyton had told him that he might be obliged to raise money by sacrificing some of his stock, and the thought brought back Clarence's uneasiness as he turned again to the trail. Indeed, he was hardly in the vein for a gentle tryst, as he entered the wooded ravine to seek the madrono tree which was to serve as a guide to his lady's bower.

A few rods further, under the cool vault filled with woodland spicing, he came upon it. In its summer harlequin dress of scarlet and green, with hanging bells of poly-tinted berries, like some personified sylvan Folly, it seemed a fitting symbol of Susy's childish masquerade of passion. Its bizarre beauty, so opposed to the sober gravity of the sedate pines and hemlocks, made it an unmistakable landmark. Here he dismounted and picketed his horse. And here, beside it, to the right, ran the little trail crawling over mossy boulders; a narrow yellow track through the carpet of pine needles between the closest file of trees; an almost imperceptible streak across pools of chickweed at their roots, and a brown and ragged swath through the ferns. As he went on, the anxiety and uneasiness that had possessed him gave way to a languid intoxication of the senses; the mysterious seclusion of these woodland depths recovered the old influence they had exerted over his boyhood. He was not returning to Susy, as much as to the older love of his youth, of which she was, perhaps, only an incident. It was therefore with an odd boyish thrill again that, coming suddenly upon a little hollow, like a deserted nest, where the lost trail made him hesitate, he heard the crackle of a starched skirt behind him, was conscious of the subtle odor of freshly ironed and scented muslin, and felt the gentle pressure of delicate fingers upon his eyes.

"Susy!"

"You silly boy! Where were you blundering to? Why didn't you look around you?"

"I thought I would hear your voices."

"Whose voices, idiot?"

"Yours and Mary's," returned Clarence innocently, looking round for the confidante.

"Oh, indeed! Then you wanted to see MARY? Well, she's looking for me somewhere. Perhaps you'll go and find her, or shall I?"

She was offering to pass him when he laid his hand on hers to detain her. She instantly evaded it, and drew herself up to her full height, incontestably displaying the dignity of the added inches to her skirt. All this was charmingly like the old Susy, but it did not bid fair to help him to a serious interview. And, looking at the pretty, pink, mocking face before him, with the witchery of the woodland still upon him, he began to think that he had better put it off.

"Never mind about Mary," he said laughingly. "But you said you wanted to see me, Susy; and here I am."

"Said I wanted to see you?" repeated Susy, with her blue eyes lifted in celestial scorn and wonderment. "Said I wanted to see you? Are you not mistaken, Mr. Brant? Really, I imagined that you came here to see ME."

With her fair head upturned, and the leaf of her scarlet lip temptingly curled over, Clarence began to think this latest phase of her extravagance the most fascinating. He drew nearer to her as he said gently, "You know what I mean, Susy. You said yesterday you were troubled. I thought you might have something to tell me."

"I should think it was YOU who might have something to tell me after all these years," she said poutingly, yet self-possessed. "But I suppose you came here only to see Mary and mother. I'm sure you let them know that plainly enough last evening."

"But you said"—began the stupefied Clarence.

"Never mind what I said. It's always what I say, never what YOU say; and you don't say anything."

The woodland influence must have been still very strong upon Clarence that he did not discover in all this that, while Susy's general capriciousness was unchanged, there was a new and singular insincerity in her manifest acting. She was either concealing the existence of some other real emotion, or assuming one that was absent. But he did not notice it, and only replied tenderly:—

"But I want to say a great deal to you, Susy. I want to say that if you still feel as I do, and as I have always felt, and you think you could be happy as I would be if—if—we could be always together, we need not conceal it from your mother and father any longer. I am old enough to speak for myself, and I am my own master. Your mother has been very kind to me—so kind that it doesn't seem quite right to deceive her— and when I tell her that I love you, and that I want you to be my wife, I believe she will give us her blessing."

Susy uttered a strange little laugh, and with an assumption of coyness, that was, however, still affected, stooped to pick a few berries from a manzanita bush.

"I'll tell you what she'll say, Clarence. She'll say you're frightfully young, and so you are!"

The young fellow tried to echo the laugh, but felt as if he had received a blow. For the first time he was conscious of the truth: this girl, whom he had fondly regarded as a child, had already passed him in the race; she had become a woman before he was yet a man, and now stood before him, maturer in her knowledge, and older in her understanding, of herself and of him. This was the change that had perplexed him; this was the presence that had come between them—a Susy he had never known before.

She laughed at his changed expression, and then swung herself easily to a sitting posture on the low projecting branch of a hemlock. The act was still girlish, but, never- theless, she looked down upon him in a superior, patronizing way. "Now, Clarence," she said, with a half-abstracted manner, "don't you be a big fool! If you talk that way to mother, she'll only tell you to wait two or three years until you know your own mind, and she'll pack me off to that horrid school again, besides watching me like a cat every moment you are here. If you want to stay here, and see me sometimes like this, you'll just behave as you have done, and say nothing. Do you see? Perhaps you don't care to come, or are satisfied with Mary and mother. Say so, then. Goodness knows, I don't want to force you to come here."

Modest and reserved as Clarence was generally, I fear that bashfulness of approach to the other sex was not one of these indications. He walked up to Susy with appalling directness, and passed his arm around her waist. She did not move, but remained looking at him and his intruding arm with a certain critical curiosity, as if awaiting some novel sensation. At which he kissed her. She then slowly disengaged his arm, and said:—

"Really, upon my word, Clarence," in perfectly level tones, and slipped quietly to the ground.

He again caught her in his arms, encircling her disarranged hair and part of the beribboned hat hanging over her shoulder, and remained for an instant holding her thus silently and tenderly. Then she freed herself with an abstracted air, a half smile, and an unchanged color except where her soft cheek had been abraded by his coat collar.

"You're a bold, rude boy, Clarence," she said, putting back her hair quietly, and straightening the brim of her hat. "Heaven knows where you learned manners!" and then, from a safer distance, with the same critical look in her violet eyes, "I suppose you think mother would allow THAT if she knew it?"

But Clarence, now completely subjugated, with the memory of the kiss upon him and a heightened color, protested that he only wanted to make their intercourse less constrained, and to have their relations, even their engagement, recognized by her parents; still he would take her advice. Only there was always the danger that if they were discovered she would be sent back to the convent all the same, and his banishment, instead of being the probation of a few years, would be a perpetual separation.

"We could always run away, Clarence," responded the young girl calmly. "There's nothing the matter with THAT."

Clarence was startled. The idea of desolating the sad, proud, handsome Mrs. Peyton, whom he worshiped, and her kind husband, whom he was just about to serve, was so grotesque and confusing, that he said hopelessly, "Yes."

"Of course," she continued, with the same odd affectation of coyness, which was, however, distinctly uncalled for, as she eyed him from under her broad hat, "you needn't come with me unless you like. I can run away by myself—if I want to! I've thought of it before. One can't stand everything!"

"But, Susy," said Clarence, with a swift remorseful recollection of her confidence yesterday, "is there really anything troubles you? Tell me, dear. What is it?"

"Oh, nothing—EVERYTHING! It's no use—YOU can't understand! YOU like it, I know you do. I can see it; it's your style. But it's stupid, it's awful, Clarence! With mamma snooping over you and around you all day, with her 'dear child,' 'mamma's pet,' and 'What is it, dear?' and 'Tell it all to your own mamma,' as if I would! And 'my own mamma,' indeed! As if I didn't know, Clarence, that she ISN'T. And papa, caring for nothing but this hideous, dreary rancho, and the huge, empty plains. It's worse than school, for there, at least, when you went out, you could see something besides cattle and horses and yellow-faced half-breeds! But here—Lord! it's only a wonder I haven't run away before!"

Startled and shocked as Clarence was at this revelation, accompanied as it was by a hardness of manner that was new to him, the influence of the young girl was still so strong upon him that he tried to evade it as only an extravagance, and said with a faint smile, "But where would you run to?"

She looked at him cunningly, with her head on one side, and then said:—

"I have friends, and"—

She hesitated, pursing up her pretty lips.

"And what?"

"Relations."

"Relations?"

"Yes—an aunt by marriage. She lives in Sacramento. She'd be overjoyed to have me come to her. Her second husband has a theatre there."

"But, Susy, what does Mrs. Peyton know of this?"

"Nothing. Do you think I'd tell her, and have her buy them up as she has my other relations? Do you suppose I don't know that I've been bought up like a nigger?"

She looked indignant, compressing her delicate little nostrils, and yet, somehow, Clarence had the same singular impresssion that she was only acting.

The calling of a far-off voice came faintly through the wood.

"That's Mary, looking for me," said Susy composedly. "You

must go, now, Clarence. Quick! Remember what I said—and don't breathe a word of this. Good-by."

But Clarence was standing still, breathless, hopelessly disturbed, and irresolute. Then he turned away mechanically towards the trail.

"Well, Clarence?"

She was looking at him half reproachfully, half coquettishly, with smiling, parted lips. He hastened to forget himself and his troubles upon them twice and thrice. Then she quickly disengaged herself, whispered, "Go, now," and, as Mary's call was repeated, Clarence heard her voice, high and clear, answering, "Here, dear," as he was plunging into the thicket.

He had scarcely reached the madrono tree again and remounted his horse, before he heard the sound of hoofs approaching from the road. In his present uneasiness he did not care to be discovered so near the rendezvous, and drew back into the shadow until the horseman should pass. It was Peyton, with a somewhat disturbed face, riding rapidly. Still less was he inclined to join or immediately follow him, but he was relieved when his host, instead of taking the direct road to the rancho, through the wild oats, turned off in the direction of the corral.

A moment later Clarence wheeled into the direct road, and presently found himself in the long afternoon shadows through the thickest of the grain. He was riding slowly, immersed in thought, when he was suddenly startled by a hissing noise at his ear, and what seemed to be the uncoiling stroke of a leaping serpent at his side. Instinctively he threw himself forward on his horse's neck, and as the animal shied into the grain, felt the crawling scrape and jerk of a horsehair lariat across his back and down his horse's flanks. He reined in indignantly and stood up in his stirrups. Nothing was to be seen above the level of the grain. Beneath him the trailing riata had as noiselessly vanished as if it had been indeed a gliding snake. Had he been the victim of a practical joke, or of the blunder of some stupid vacquero? For he made no doubt that it was the lasso of one of the performers he had watched that afternoon. But his preoccupied mind did not dwell long upon it, and by the time he had reached the wall of the old garden, the incident was forgotten.

CHAPTER VI

Relieved of Clarence Brant's embarrassing presence, Jim Hooker did not, however, refuse to avail himself of that opportunity to expound to the farmer and his family the immense wealth, influence, and importance of the friend who had just left him. Although Clarence's plan had suggested reticence, Hooker could not forego the pleasure of informing them that "Clar" Brant had just offered to let him into an extensive land speculation. He had previously declined a large share or original location in a mine of Clarence's, now worth a million, because it was not "his style." But the land speculation in a country of unsettled titles and lawless men, he need not remind them, required some experience of border warfare. He would not say positively, although he left them to draw their own conclusions with gloomy significance, that this was why Clarence had sought him. With this dark suggestion, he took leave of Mr. and Mrs. Hopkins and their daughter Phoebe the next day, not without some natural human emotion, and peacefully drove his team and wagon into the settlement of Fair Plains.

He was not prepared, however, for a sudden realization of his imaginative prospects. A few days after his arrival in Fair Plains, he received a letter from Clarence, explaining that he had not time to return to Hooker to consult him, but had, nevertheless, fulfilled his promise, by taking advantage of an opportunity of purchasing the Spanish "Sisters'" title to certain unoccupied lands near the settlement. As these lands in part joined the section already preempted and occupied by Hopkins, Clarence thought that Jim Hooker would choose that part for the sake of his neighbor's company. He inclosed a draft on San Francisco, for a sum sufficient to enable Jim to put up a cabin and "stock" the property, which he begged he would consider in the light of a loan, to be paid back in installments, only when the property could afford it. At the same time, if Jim was in difficulty, he was to inform him. The letter closed with a characteristic Clarence-like mingling of enthusiasm and older wisdom. "I wish you luck, Jim, but I see no reason why you should trust to it. I don't know of anything that could keep you from making yourself independent of any one, if you go to work with a LONG AIM and don't fritter away your chances on short ones. If I were you, old fellow, I'd drop the Plains and the Indians out of my thoughts, or at least out of my TALK, for a while; they won't help you in the long run. The people who believe you will be jealous of you; those who don't, will look down upon you, and if they get to questioning your little Indian romances, Jim, they'll be apt to question your civilized facts. That won't help you in the ranching business and that's your only real grip now." For the space of two or three hours after this, Jim was reasonably grateful and even subdued—so much so that his employer, to whom he confided his good fortune, frankly confessed that he believed him from that unusual fact alone. Unfortunately, neither the practical lesson conveyed in this grim admission, nor the sentiment of gratitude, remained long with Jim. Another idea had taken possession of his fancy. Although the land nominated in his bill of sale had been, except on the occasion of his own temporary halt there, always unoccupied, unsought, and unclaimed, and although he was amply protected by legal certificates, he gravely collected a posse of three or four idlers from Fair Plains, armed them at his own expense, and in the dead of night took belligerent and forcible possession of the peaceful domain which the weak generosity and unheroic dollars of Clarence had purchased for him! A martial camp-fire tempered the chill night winds to the pulses of the invaders, and enabled them to sleep on their arms in the field they had won. The morning sun revealed to the astonished Hopkins family the embattled plain beyond, with its armed sentries. Only then did Jim hooker condescend to explain the reason of his warlike occupation, with dark hints of the outlying "squatters" and "jumpers," whose incursions their boldness alone had repulsed. The effect of this romantic situation upon the two women, with the slight fascination of danger imported into their quiet lives, may well be imagined. Possibly owing to some incautious questioning by Mr. Hopkins, and some doubts of the discipline and sincerity of his posse, Jim discharged them the next day; but during the erection of his cabin by some peaceful carpenters from the settlement, he returned to his gloomy preoccupation and the ostentatious wearing of his revolvers. As an opulent and powerful neighbor, he took his meals with the family while his house was being built, and generally impressed them with a sense of security they had never missed.

Meantime, Clarence, duly informed of the installation of Jim as his tenant, underwent a severe trial. It was necessary for his plans that this should be kept a secret at present, and this was no easy thing for his habitually frank and open nature. He had once mentioned that he had met Jim at the settlement, but the information was received with such indifference by Susy, and such marked disfavor by Mrs. Peyton, that he said no more. He accompanied Peyton in his rides around the rancho, fully possessed himself of the details of its boundaries, the debatable lands held by the enemy, and listened with beating pulses, but a hushed tongue, to his host's ill-concealed misgivings.

"You see, Clarence, that lower terrace?" he said, pointing to a far-reaching longitudinal plain beyond the corral; "it extends from my corral to Fair Plains. That is claimed by the sisters' title, and, as things appear to be going, if a division of the land is made it will be theirs. It's bad enough to have this best grazing land lying just on the flanks of the corral held by these rascals at an absurd prohibitory price, but I am afraid that it may be made to mean something even worse. According to the old surveys, these terraces on different levels were the natural divisions of the property— one heir or his tenant taking one, and another taking another—an easy distinction that saved the necessity of boundary fencing or monuments, and gave no trouble to people who were either kinsmen or lived in lazy patriarchal concord. That is the form of division they are trying to reestablish now. Well," he continued, suddenly lifting his eyes to the young man's flushed face, in some unconscious, sympathetic response to his earnest breathlessness, "although my boundary line extends half a mile into that field, my house and garden and corral ARE ACTUALLY UPON THAT TERRACE OR LEVEL." They certainly appeared to Clarence to be on the same line as the long field beyond. "If," went on Peyton, "such a decision is made, these men will push on and claim the house and everything on the terrace."

"But," said Clarence quickly, "you said their title was only valuable where they have got or can give POSSESSION. You already have yours. They can't take it from you except by force."

"No," said Peyton grimly, "nor will they dare to do it as long as I live to fight them."

"But," persisted Clarence, with the same singular hesitancy of manner, "why didn't you purchase possession of at least that part of the land which lies so dangerously near your own house?"

"Because it was held by squatters, who naturally preferred buying what might prove a legal title to their land from these impostors than to sell out their possession to ME at a fair price."

"But couldn't you have bought from them both?" continued Clarence.

"My dear Clarence, I am not a Croesus nor a fool. Only a man who was both would attempt to treat with these rascals, who would now, of course, insist that THEIR WHOLE claim should be bought up at their own price, by the man who was most concerned in defeating them."

He turned away a little impatiently. Fortunately he did not observe that Clarence's averted face was crimson with embarrassment, and that a faint smile hovered nervously about his mouth.

Since his late rendezvous with Susy, Clarence had had no chance to interrogate her further regarding her mysterious relative. That that shadowy presence was more or less exaggerated, if not an absolute myth, he more than half suspected, but of the discontent that had produced it, or the recklessness it might provoke, there was no doubt. She might be tempted to some act of folly. He wondered if Mary Rogers knew it. Yet, with his sensitive ideas of loyalty, he would have shrunk from any confidence with Mary regarding her friend's secrets, although he fancied that Mary's dark eyes sometimes dwelt upon him with mournful consciousness and premonition. He did not imagine the truth, that this romantic contemplation was only the result of Mary's conviction that Susy was utterly unworthy of his love. It so chanced one morning that the vacquero who brought the post from Santa Inez arrived earlier than usual, and so anticipated the two girls, who usually made a youthful point of meeting him first as he passed the garden wall. The letter bag was consequently delivered to Mrs. Peyton in the presence of the others, and a look of consternation passed between the young girls. But Mary quickly seized upon the bag as if with girlish and mischievous impatience, opened it, and glanced within it.

"There are only three letters for you," she said, handing them to Clarence, with a quick look of significance, which he failed to comprehend, "and nothing for me or Susy."

"But," began the innocent Clarence, as his first glance at the letters showed him that one was directed to Susy, "here is"—

A wicked pinch on his arm that was nearest Mary stopped his speech, and he quickly put the letters in his pocket.

"Didn't you understand that Susy don't want her mother to see that letter?" asked Mary impatiently, when they were alone a moment later.

"No," said Clarence simply, handing her the missive.

Mary took it and turned it over in her hands.

"It's in a man's handwriting," she said innocently.

"I hadn't noticed it," returned Clarence with invincible naivete, "but perhaps it is."

"And you hand it over for me to give to Susy, and ain't a bit curious to know who it's from?"

"No," returned Clarence, opening his big eyes in smiling and apologetic wonder.

"Well," responded the young lady, with a long breath of melancholy astonishment, "certainly, of all things you are— you really ARE!" With which incoherency—apparently perfectly intelligible to herself—she left him. She had not herself the slightest idea who the letter was from; she only knew that Susy wanted it concealed.

The incident made little impression on Clarence, except as part of the general uneasiness he felt in regard to his old playmate. It seemed so odd to him that this worry should come from HER—that she herself should form the one discordant note in the Arcadian dream that he had found so sweet; in his previous imaginings it was the presence of Mrs. Peyton which he had dreaded; she whose propinquity now seemed so full of gentleness, reassurance, and repose. How worthy she seemed of any sacrifice he could make for her! He had seen little of her for the last two or three days, although her smile and greeting were always ready for him. Poor Clarence did not dream that she had found from certain incontestable signs and tokens, both in the young ladies and himself, that he did not require watching, and that becoming more resigned to Susy's indifference, which seemed so general and passive in quality, she was no longer tortured by the sting of jealousy.

Finding himself alone that afternoon, the young man had wandered somewhat listlessly beyond the low adobe gateway. The habits of the siesta obtained in a modified form at the rancho. After luncheon, its masters and employees usually retired, not so much from the torrid heat of the afternoon sun, but from the first harrying of the afternoon trades, whose monotonous whistle swept round the walls. A straggling passion vine near the gate beat and struggled against the wind. Clarence had stopped near it, and was gazing with worried abstraction across the tossing fields, when a soft voice called his name.

It was a pleasant voice—Mrs. Peyton's. He glanced back at the gateway; it was empty. He looked quickly to the right and left; no one was there.

The voice spoke again with the musical addition of a laugh; it seemed to come from the passion vine. Ah, yes; behind it, and half overgrown by its branches, was a long, narrow embrasured opening in the wall, defended by the usual Spanish grating, and still further back, as in the frame of a picture, the half length figure of Mrs. Peyton, very handsome and striking, too, with a painted picturesqueness from the effect of the checkered light and shade.

"You looked so tired and bored out there," she said. "I am afraid you are finding it very dull at the rancho. The prospect is certainly not very enlivening from where you stand."

Clarence protested with a visible pleasure in his eyes, as he held back a spray before the opening.

"If you are not afraid of being worse bored, come in here and talk with me. You have never seen this part of the house, I think—my own sitting-room. You reach it from the hall in the gallery. But Lola or Anita will show you the way."

He reentered the gateway, and quickly found the hall—a narrow, arched passage, whose black, tunnel-like shadows were absolutely unaffected by the vivid, colorless glare of the courtyard without, seen through an opening at the end. The contrast was sharp, blinding, and distinct; even the edges of the opening were black; the outer light halted on the threshold and never penetrated within. The warm odor of verbena and dried rose leaves stole from a half-open door somewhere in the cloistered gloom. Guided by it, Clarence presently found himself on the threshold of a low-vaulted room. Two other narrow embrasured windows like the one he had just seen, and a fourth, wider latticed casement, hung with gauze curtains, suffused the apartment with a clear, yet mysterious twilight that seemed its own. The gloomy walls were warmed by bright-fringed bookshelves, topped with trifles of light feminine coloring and adornment. Low easy-chairs and a lounge, small fanciful tables, a dainty desk, gayly colored baskets of worsteds or mysterious kaleido-scopic fragments, and vases of flowers pervaded the apartment with a mingled sense of grace and comfort. There was a womanly refinement in its careless negligence, and even the delicate wrapper of Japanese silk, gathered at the waist and falling in easy folds to the feet of the graceful mistress of this charming disorder, looked a part of its refined abandonment.

Clarence hesitated as on the threshold of some sacred shrine. But Mrs. Peyton, with her own hands, cleared a space for him on the lounge.

"You will easily suspect from all this disorder, Mr. Brant, that I spend a greater part of my time here, and that I seldom see much company. Mr. Peyton occasionally comes in long enough to stumble over a footstool or upset a vase, and I think Mary and Susy avoid it from a firm conviction that there is work concealed in these baskets. But I have my books here, and in the afternoons, behind these thick walls, one forgets the incessant stir and restlessness of the dreadful winds outside. Just now you were foolish enough to tempt them while you were nervous, or worried, or listless. Take my word for it, it's a great mistake. There is no more use fighting them, as I tell Mr. Peyton, than of fighting the people born under them. I have my own opinion that these winds were sent only to stir this lazy race of mongrels into activity, but they are enough to drive us Anglo-Saxons into nervous frenzy. Don't you think so? But you are young and energetic, and perhaps you are not affected by them."

She spoke pleasantly and playfully, yet with a certain nervous tension of voice and manner that seemed to illustrate her theory. At least, Clarence, in quick sympathy with her slightest emotion, was touched by it. There is no more insidious attraction in the persons we admire, than the belief that we know and understand their unhappiness, and that our admiration for them is lifted higher than a mere mutual instinctive sympathy with beauty or strength. This adorable woman had suffered. The very thought aroused his chivalry. It loosened, also, I fear, his quick, impulsive tongue.

Oh, yes; he knew it. He had lived under this whip of air and sky for three years, alone in a Spanish rancho, with only the native peons around him, and scarcely speaking his own tongue even to his guardian. He spent his mornings on horseback in fields like these, until the vientos generales, as they called them, sprang up and drove him nearly frantic; and his only relief was to bury himself among the books in his guardian's library, and shut out the world—just as she did. The smile which hovered around the lady's mouth at that moment arrested Clarence, with a quick remembrance of their former relative positions, and a sudden conviction of his familiarity in suggesting an equality of experience, and he blushed. But Mrs. Peyton diverted his embarrassment with an air of interested absorption in his story, and said:—

"Then you know these people thoroughly, Mr. Brant? I am afraid that WE do not."

Clarence had already gathered that fact within the last few days, and, with his usual impulsive directness, said so. A slight knitting of Mrs. Peyton's brows passed off, however, as he quickly and earnestly went on to say that it was impossible for the Peytons in their present relations to the natives to judge them, or to be judged by them fairly. How they were a childlike race, credulous and trustful, but, like all credulous and trustful people, given to retaliate when imposed upon with a larger insincerity, exaggeration, and treachery. How they had seen their houses and lands occupied by strangers, their religion scorned, their customs derided, their patriarchal society invaded by hollow civilization or frontier brutality—all this fortified by incident and illustration, the outcome of some youthful experience, and given with the glowing enthusiasm of conviction. Mrs. Peyton listened with the usual divided feminine interest between subject and speaker.

Where did this rough, sullen boy—as she had known him—pick up this delicate and swift perception, this reflective judgment, and this odd felicity of expression? It was not possible that it was in him while he was the companion of her husband's servants or the recognized "chum" of the scamp Hooker. No. But if HE could have changed like this, why not Susy? Mrs. Peyton, in the conservatism of her sex, had never been quite free from fears of her adopted daughter's hereditary instincts; but, with this example before her, she now took heart. Perhaps the change was coming slowly; perhaps even now what she thought was indifference and coldness was only some abnormal preparation or condition. But she only smiled and said:—

"Then, if you think those people have been wronged, you are not on our side, Mr. Brant?"

What to an older and more worldly man would have seemed, and probably was, only a playful reproach, struck Clarence deeply, and brought his pent-up feelings to his lips.

"YOU have never wronged them. You couldn't do it; it isn't in your nature. I am on YOUR side, and for you and yours always, Mrs. Peyton. From the first time I saw you on the plains, when I was brought, a ragged boy, before you by your husband, I think I would gladly have laid down my life for you. I don't mind telling you now that I was even jealous of poor Susy, so anxious was I for the smallest share in your thoughts, if only for a moment. You could have done anything with me you wished, and I should have been happy—far happier than I have been ever since. I tell you this, Mrs. Peyton, now, because you have just doubted if I might be 'on your side,' but I have been longing to tell it all to you before, and it is that I am ready to do anything you want—all you want—to be on YOUR SIDE and at YOUR SIDE, now and forever."

He was so earnest and hearty, and above all so appallingly and blissfully happy, in this relief of his feelings, smiling as if it were the most natural thing in the world, and so absurdly unconscious of his twenty-two years, his little brown curling mustache, the fire in his wistful, yearning eyes, and, above all, of his clasped hands and lover-like attitude, that Mrs. Peyton—at first rigid as stone, then suffused to the eyes— cast a hasty glance round the apartment, put her handkerchief to her face, and laughed like a girl.

At which Clarence, by no means discomposed, but rather accepting her emotion as perfectly natural, joined her heartily, and added:—

"It's so, Mrs. Peyton; I'm glad I told you. You don't mind it, do you?"

But Mrs. Peyton had resumed her gravity, and perhaps a touch of her previous misgivings.

"I should certainly be very sorry," she said, looking at him critically, "to object to your sharing your old friendship for your little playmate with her parents and guardians, or to your expressing it to THEM as frankly as to her."

She saw the quick change in his mobile face and the momentary arrest of its happy expression. She was frightened and yet puzzled. It was not the sensitiveness of a lover at the mention of the loved one's name, and yet it suggested an uneasy consciousness. If his previous impulsive outburst had been prompted honestly, or even artfully, by his passion for Susy, why had he looked so shocked when she spoke of her?

But Clarence, whose emotion had been caused by the sudden recall of his knowledge of Susy's own disloyalty to the woman whose searching eyes were upon him, in his revulsion against the deceit was, for an instant, upon the point of divulging all. Perhaps, if Mrs. Peyton had shown more confidence, he would have done so, and materially altered the evolution of this story. But, happily, it is upon these slight human weaknesses that your romancer depends, and Clarence, with no other reason than the instinctive sympathy of youth with youth in its opposition to wisdom and experience, let the opportunity pass, and took the responsibility of it out of the hands of this chronicler.

Howbeit, to cover his confusion, he seized upon the second idea that was in his mind, and stammered, "Susy! Yes, I wanted to speak to you about her." Mrs. Peyton held her breath, but the young man went on, although hesitatingly, with evident sincerity. "Have you heard from any of her relations since—since—you adopted her?"

It seemed a natural enough question, although not the sequitur she had expected. "No," she said carelessly. "It was well understood, after the nearest relation—an aunt by marriage—had signed her consent to Susy's adoption, that there should be no further intercourse with the family. There seemed to us no necessity for reopening the past, and Susy herself expressed no desire." She stopped, and again fixing her handsome eyes on Clarence, said, "Do you know any of them?"

But Clarence by this time had recovered himself, and was able to answer carelessly and truthfully that he did not. Mrs. Peyton, still regarding him closely, added somewhat deliberately, "It matters little now what relations she has; Mr. Peyton and I have complete legal control over her until she is of age, and we can easily protect her from any folly of her own or others, or from any of the foolish fancies that sometimes overtake girls of her age and inexperience."

To her utter surprise, however, Clarence uttered a faint sigh of relief, and his face again recovered its expression of boyish happiness. "I'm glad of it, Mrs. Peyton," he said heartily. "No one could understand better what is for her interest in all things than yourself. Not," he said, with hasty and equally hearty loyalty to his old playmate, "that I think she would ever go against your wishes, or do anything that she knows to be wrong, but she is very young and innocent—as much of a child as ever, don't you think so, Mrs. Peyton?"

It was amusing, yet nevertheless puzzling, to hear this boyish young man comment upon Susy's girlishness. And Clarence was serious, for he had quite forgotten in Mrs. Peyton's presence the impression of superiority which Susy had lately made upon him. But Mrs. Peyton returned to the charge, or, rather, to an attack upon what she conceived to be Clarence's old position.

"I suppose she does seem girlish compared to Mary Rogers, who is a much more reserved and quiet nature. But Mary is very charming, Mr. Brant, and I am really delighted to have her here with Susy. She has such lovely dark eyes and such good manners. She has been well brought up, and it is easy to see that her friends are superior people. I must write to them to thank them for her visit, and beg them to let her stay longer. I think you said you didn't know them?"

But Clarence, whose eyes had been thoughtfully and admiringly wandering over every characteristic detail of the charming apartment, here raised them to its handsome mistress, with an apologetic air and a "No" of such unaffected and complete abstraction, that she was again dumbfounded. Certainly, it could not be Mary in whom he was interested.

Abandoning any further inquisition for the present, she let the talk naturally fall upon the books scattered about the tables. The young man knew them all far better than she did, with a cognate knowledge of others of which she had never heard. She found herself in the attitude of receiving information from this boy, whose boyishness, however, seemed to have evaporated, whose tone had changed with the subject, and who now spoke with the conscious reserve of knowledge. Decidedly, she must have grown rusty in her seclusion. This came, she thought bitterly, of living alone; of her husband's preoccupation with the property; of Susy's frivolous caprices. At the end of eight years to be outstripped by a former cattle-boy of her husband's, and to have her French corrected in a matter of fact way by this recent pupil of the priests, was really too bad! Perhaps he even looked down upon Susy! She smiled dangerously but suavely.

"You must have worked so hard to educate yourself from nothing, Mr. Brant. You couldn't read, I think, when you first came to us. No? Could you really? I know it has been very difficult for Susy to get on with her studies in proportion. We had so much to first eradicate in the way of manners, style, and habits of thought which the poor child had picked up from her companions, and for which SHE was not responsible. Of course, with a boy that does not signify," she added, with feline gentleness.

But the barbed speech glanced from the young man's smoothly smiling abstraction.

"Ah, yes. But those were happy days, Mrs. Peyton," he answered, with an exasperating return of his previous boyish enthusiasm, "perhaps because of our ignorance. I don't think that Susy and I are any happier for knowing that the plains are not as flat as we believed they were, and that the sun doesn't have to burn a hole in them every night when it sets. But I know I believed that YOU knew everything. When I once saw you smiling over a book in your hand, I thought it must be a different one from any that I had ever seen, and perhaps made expressly for you. I can see you there still. Do you know," quite confidentially, "that you reminded me—of course YOU were much younger—of what I remembered of my mother?"

But Mrs. Peyton's reply of "Ah, indeed," albeit polite, indicated some coldness and lack of animation. Clarence rose quickly, but cast a long and lingering look around him.

"You will come again, Mr. Brant," said the lady more graciously. "If you are going to ride now, perhaps you would try to meet Mr. Peyton. He is late already, and I am always uneasy when he is out alone—particularly on one of those half-broken horses, which they consider good enough for riding here. YOU have ridden them before and understand them, but I am afraid that's another thing WE have got to learn."

When the young man found himself again confronting the glittering light of the courtyard, he remembered the interview and the soft twilight of the boudoir only as part of a pleasant dream. There was a rude awakening in the fierce wind, which had increased with the lengthening shadows. It seemed to sweep away the half-sensuous comfort that had pervaded him, and made him coldly realize that he had done nothing to solve the difficulties of his relations to Susy. He had lost the one chance of confiding to Mrs. Peyton—if he had ever really intended to do so. It was impossible for him to do it hereafter without a confession of prolonged deceit.

He reached the stables impatiently, where his attention was attracted by the sound of excited voices in the corral. Looking within, he was concerned to see that one of the vacqueros was holding the dragging bridle of a blown, dusty, and foam-covered horse, around whom a dozen idlers were gathered. Even beneath its coating of dust and foam and the half-displaced saddle blanket, Clarence immediately recognized the spirited pinto mustang which Peyton had ridden that morning.

"What's the matter?" said Clarence, from the gateway.

The men fell apart, glancing at each other. One said quickly in Spanish:—

"Say nothing to HIM. It is an affair of the house."

But this brought Clarence down like a bombshell among them, not to be overlooked in his equal command of their tongue and of them. "Ah! come, now. What drunken piggishness is this? Speak!"

"The padron has been—perhaps—thrown," stammered the first speaker. "His horse arrives—but he does not. We go to inform the senora."

"No, you don't! mules and imbeciles! Do you want to frighten her to death? Mount, every one of you, and follow me!"

The men hesitated, but for only a moment. Clarence had a fine assortment of Spanish epithets, expletives, and objurgations, gathered in his rodeo experience at El Refugio, and laid them about him with such fervor and discrimination that two or three mules, presumably with guilty consciences, mistaking their direction, actually cowered against the stockade of the corral in fear. In another moment the vacqueros had hastily mounted, and, with Clarence at their head, were dashing down the road towards Santa Inez. Here he spread them in open order in the grain, on either side of the track, himself taking the road.

They did not proceed very far. For when they had reached the gradual slope which marked the decline to the second terrace, Clarence, obeying an instinct as irresistible as it was unaccountable, which for the last few moments had been forcing itself upon him, ordered a halt. The casa and corral had already sunk in the plain behind them; it was the spot where the lasso had been thrown at him a few evenings before! Bidding the men converge slowly towards the road, he went on more cautiously, with his eyes upon the track before him. Presently he stopped. There was a ragged displacement of the cracked and crumbling soil and the unmistakable scoop of kicking hoofs. As he stooped to examine them, one of the men at the right uttered a shout. By the same strange instinct Clarence knew that Peyton was found!

Bret Harte

He was, indeed, lying there among the wild oats at the right of the road, but without trace of life or scarcely human appearance. His clothes, where not torn and shredded away, were partly turned inside out; his shoulders, neck, and head were a shapeless, undistinguishable mask of dried earth and rags, like a mummy wrapping. His left boot was gone. His large frame seemed boneless, and, except for the cerements of his mud-stiffened clothing, was limp and sodden.

Clarence raised his head suddenly from a quick examination of the body, and looked at the men around him. One of them was already cantering away. Clarence instantly threw himself on his horse, and, putting spurs to the animal, drew a revolver from his holster and fired over the man's head. The rider turned in his saddle, saw his pursuer, and pulled up.

"Go back," said Clarence, "or my next shot won't MISS you."

"I was only going to inform the senora," said the man with a shrug and a forced smile.

"I will do that," said Clarence grimly, driving him back with him into the waiting circle; then turning to them he said slowly, with deliberate, smileless irony, "And now, my brave gentlemen—knights of the bull and gallant mustang hunters—I want to inform YOU that I believe that Mr. Peyton was MURDERED, and if the man who killed him is anywhere this side of hell, I intend to find him. Good! You understand me! Now lift up the body—you two, by the shoulders; you two, by the feet. Let your horses follow. For I intend that you four shall carry home your master in your arms, on foot. Now forward to the corral by the back trail. Disobey me, or step out of line and"—He raised the revolver ominously.

If the change wrought in the dead man before them was weird and terrifying, no less distinct and ominous was the change that, during the last few minutes, had come over the living speaker. For it was no longer the youthful Clarence who sat there, but a haggard, prematurely worn, desperate-looking avenger, lank of cheek, and injected of eye, whose white teeth glistened under the brown mustache and thin pale lips that parted when his restrained breath now and then hurriedly escaped them.

As the procession moved on, two men slunk behind with the horses.

"Mother of God! Who is this wolf's whelp?" said Manuel.

"Hush!" said his companion in a terrified whisper. "Have you not heard? It is the son of Hamilton Brant, the assassin, the duelist—he who was fusiladed in Sonora." He made the sign of the cross quickly. "Jesus Maria! Let them look out who have cause, for the blood of his father is in him!"

CHAPTER VII

What other speech passed between Clarence and Peyton's retainers was not known, but not a word of the interview seemed to have been divulged by those present. It was generally believed and accepted that Judge Peyton met his death by being thrown from his half-broken mustang, and dragged at its heels, and medical opinion, hastily summoned from Santa Inez after the body had been borne to the corral, and stripped of its hideous encasings, declared that the neck had been broken, and death had followed instantaneously. An inquest was deemed unnecessary.

Clarence had selected Mary to break the news to Mrs. Peyton, and the frightened young girl was too much struck with the change still visible in his face, and the half authority of his manner, to decline, or even to fully appreciate the calamity that had befallen them. After the first benumbing shock, Mrs. Peyton passed into that strange exaltation of excitement brought on by the immediate necessity for action, followed by a pallid calm, which the average spectator too often unfairly accepts as incongruous, inadequate, or artificial. There had also occurred one of those strange compensations that wait on Death or disrupture by catastrophe: such as the rude shaking down of an unsettled life, the forcible realization of what were vague speculations, the breaking of old habits and traditions, and the unloosing of half-conscious bonds. Mrs. Peyton, without insensibility to her loss or disloyalty to her affections, nevertheless felt a relief to know that she was now really Susy's guardian, free to order her new life wherever and under what conditions she chose as most favorable to it, and that she could dispose of this house that was wearying to her when Susy was away, and which the girl herself had always found insupportable. She could settle this question of Clarence's relations to her daughter out of hand without advice or opposition. She had a brother in the East, who would be summoned to take care of the property. This consideration for the living pursued her, even while the dead man's presence still awed the hushed house; it was in her thoughts as she stood beside his bier and adjusted the flowers on his breast, which no longer moved for or against these vanities; and it stayed with her even in the solitude of her darkened room.

But if Mrs. Peyton was deficient, it was Susy who filled the popular idea of a mourner, and whose emotional attitude of a grief-stricken daughter left nothing to be desired. It was she who, when the house was filled with sympathizing friends from San Francisco and the few near neighbors who had hurried with condolences, was overflowing in her reminiscences of the dead man's goodness to her, and her own undying affection; who recalled ominous things that he had said, and strange premonitions of her own, the result of her ever-present filial anxiety; it was she who had hurried home that afternoon, impelled with vague fears of some impending calamity; it was she who drew a picture of Peyton as a doting and almost too indulgent parent, which Mary Rogers failed to recognize, and which brought back vividly to Clarence's recollection her own childish exaggerations of the Indian massacre. I am far from saying that she was entirely insincere or merely acting at these moments; at times she was taken with a mild hysteria, brought on by the exciting intrusion of this real event in her monotonous life, by the attentions of her friends, the importance of her suffering as an only child, and the advancement of her position as the heiress of the Robles Rancho. If her tears were near the surface, they were at least genuine, and filmed her violet eyes and reddened her pretty eyelids quite as effectually as if they had welled from the depths of her being. Her black frock lent a matured dignity to her figure, and paled her delicate complexion with the refinement of suffering. Even Clarence was moved in that dark and haggard abstraction that had settled upon him since his strange outbreak over the body of his old friend.

The extent of that change had not been noticed by Mrs. Peyton, who had only observed that Clarence had treated her grief with a grave and silent respect. She was grateful for that. A repetition of his boyish impulsiveness would have been distasteful to her at such a moment. She only thought him more mature and more subdued, and as the only man now in her household his services had been invaluable in the emergency.

The funeral had taken place at Santa Inez, where half the county gathered to pay their last respects to their former fellow-citizen and neighbor, whose legal and combative victories they had admired, and whom death had lifted into a public character. The family were returning to the house the same afternoon, Mrs. Peyton and the girls in one carriage, the female house-servants in another, and Clarence on horseback. They had reached the first plateau, and Clarence was riding a little in advance, when an extraordinary figure, rising from the grain beyond, began to gesticulate to him wildly. Checking the driver of the first carriage, Clarence bore down upon the stranger. To his amazement it was Jim Hooker. Mounted on a peaceful, unwieldy plough horse, he was nevertheless accoutred and armed after his most extravagant fashion. In addition to a heavy rifle across his saddle-bow he was weighted down with a knife and revolvers. Clarence was in no mood for trifling, and almost rudely demanded his business.

"Gord, Clarence, it ain't foolin'. The Sisters' title was decided yesterday."

"I knew it, you fool! It's YOUR title! You were already on your land and in possession. What the devil are you doing HERE?"

"Yes—but," stammered Jim, "all the boys holding that title moved up here to 'make the division' and grab all they could. And I followed. And I found out that they were going to grab Judge Peyton's house, because it was on the line, if they could, and findin' you was all away, by Gord THEY DID! and they're in it! And I stoled out and rode down here to warn ye."

He stopped, looked at Clarence, glanced darkly around him and then down on his accoutrements. Even in that supreme moment of sincerity, he could not resist the possibilities of the situation.

"It's as much as my life's worth," he said gloomily. "But," with a dark glance at his weapons, "I'll sell it dearly."

"Jim!" said Clarence, in a terrible voice, "you're not lying again?"

"No," said Jim hurriedly. "I swear it, Clarence! No! Honest Injin this time. And look. I'll help you. They ain't expectin' you yet, and they think ye'll come by the road. Ef I raised a scare off there by the corral, while you're creepin' ROUND BY THE BACK, mebbe you could get in while they're all lookin' for ye in front, don't you see? I'll raise a big row, and they needn't know but what ye've got wind of it and brought a party with you from Santa Inez."

In a flash Clarence had wrought a feasible plan out of Jim's fantasy.

"Good," he said, wringing his old companion's hand. "Go back quietly now; hang round the corral, and when you see the carriage climbing the last terrace raise your alarm. Don't mind how loud it is, there'll be nobody but the servants in the carriages."

He rode quickly back to the first carriage, at whose window Mrs. Peyton's calm face was already questioning him. He told her briefly and concisely of the attack, and what he proposed to do.

"You have shown yourself so strong in matters of worse moment than this," he added quietly, "that I have no fears for your courage. I have only to ask you to trust yourself to me, to put you back at once in your own home. Your presence there, just now, is the one important thing, whatever happens afterwards."

She recognized his maturer tone and determined manner, and nodded assent. More than that, a faint fire came into her handsome eyes; the two girls kindled their own at that flaming beacon, and sat with flushed checks and suspended, indignant breath. They were Western Americans, and not over much used to imposition.

"You must get down before we raise the hill, and follow me on foot through the grain. I was thinking," he added, turning to Mrs. Peyton, "of your boudoir window."

She had been thinking of it, too, and nodded.

"The vine has loosened the bars," he said.

"If it hasn't, we must squeeze through them," she returned simply.

At the end of the terrace Clarence dismounted, and helped them from the carriage. He then gave directions to the coachmen to follow the road slowly to the corral in front of the casa, and tied his horse behind the second carriage. Then, with Mrs. Peyton and the two young girls, he plunged into the grain.

It was hot, it was dusty, their thin shoes slipped in the crumbling adobe, and the great blades caught in their crape draperies, but they uttered no complaint. Whatever ulterior thought was in their minds, they were bent only on one thing at that moment—on entering the house at any hazard. Mrs. Peyton had lived long enough on the frontier to know the magic power of POSSESSION. Susy already was old enough to feel the acute feminine horror of the profanation of her own belongings by alien hands. Clarence, more cognizant of the whole truth than the others, was equally silent and determined; and Mary Rogers was fired with the zeal of loyalty.

Suddenly a series of blood-curdling yells broke from the direction of the corral, and they stopped. But Clarence at once recognized the well-known war-whoop imitation of Jim Hooker—infinitely more gruesome and appalling than the genuine aboriginal challenge. A half dozen shots fired in quick succession had evidently the same friendly origin.

"Now is our time," said Clarence eagerly. "We must run for the house."

They had fortunately reached by this time the angle of the

adobe wall of the casa, and the long afternoon shadows of the building were in their favor. They pressed forward eagerly with the sounds of Jim Hooker's sham encounter still in their ears, mingled with answering shouts of defiance from strange voices within the building towards the front.

They rapidly skirted the wall, even passing boldly before the back gateway, which seemed empty and deserted, and the next moment stood beside the narrow window of the boudoir. Clarence's surmises were correct; the iron grating was not only loose, but yielded to a vigorous wrench, the vine itself acting as a lever to pull out the rusty bars. The young man held out his hand, but Mrs. Peyton, with the sudden agility of a young girl, leaped into the window, followed by Mary and Susy. The inner casement yielded to her touch; the next moment they were within the room. Then Mrs. Peyton's flushed and triumphant face reappeared at the window.

"It's all right; the men are all in the courtyard, or in the front of the house. The boudoir door is strong, and we can bolt them out."

"It won't be necessary," said Clarence quietly; "you will not be disturbed."

"But are you not coming in?" she asked timidly, holding the window open.

Clarence looked at her with his first faint smile since Peyton's death.

"Of course I am, but not in THAT way. I am going in by THE FRONT GATE."

She would have detained him, but, with a quick wave of his

hand, he left her, and ran swiftly around the wall of the casa toward the front. The gate was half open; a dozen excited men were gathered before it and in the archway, and among them, whitened with dust, blackened with powder, and apparently glutted with rapine, and still holding a revolver in his hand, was Jim Hooker! As Clarence approached, the men quickly retreated inside the gate and closed it, but not before he had exchanged a meaning glance with Jim. When he reached the gate, a man from within roughly demanded his business.

"I wish to see the leader of this party," said Clarence quietly.

"I reckon you do," returned the man, with a short laugh. "But I kalkilate HE don't return the compliment."

"He probably will when he reads this note to his employer," continued Clarence still coolly, selecting a paper from his pocketbook. It was addressed to Francisco Robles, Superintendent of the Sisters' Title, and directed him to give Mr. Clarence Brant free access to the property and the fullest information concerning it. The man took it, glanced at it, looked again at Clarence, and then passed the paper to a third man among the group in the courtyard. The latter read it, and approached the gate carelessly.

"Well, what do you want?"

"I am afraid you have the advantage of me in being able to transact business through bars," said Clarence, with slow but malevolent distinctness, "and as mine is important, I think you had better open the gate to me."

The slight laugh that his speech had evoked from the bystanders was checked as the leader retorted angrily:—

"That's all very well; but how do I know that you're the man represented in that letter? Pancho Robles may know you, but I don't."

"That you can find out very easily," said Clarence. "There is a man among your party who knows me—Mr. Hooker. Ask him."

The man turned, with a quick mingling of surprise and suspicion, to the gloomy, imperturbable Hooker. Clarence could not hear the reply of that young gentleman, but it was evidently not wanting in his usual dark, enigmatical exaggeration. The man surlily opened the gate.

"All the same," he said, still glancing suspiciously at Hooker, "I don't see what HE'S got to do with you."

"A great deal," said Clarence, entering the courtyard, and stepping into the veranda; "HE'S ONE OF MY TENANTS."

"Your WHAT?" said the man, with a coarse laugh of incredulity.

"My tenants," repeated Clarence, glancing around the courtyard carelessly. Nevertheless, he was relieved to notice that the three or four Mexicans of the party did not seem to be old retainers of the rancho. There was no evidence of the internal treachery he had feared.

"Your TENANTS!" echoed the man, with an uneasy glance at the faces of the others.

"Yes," said Clarence, with business brevity; "and, for the matter of that, although I have no reason to be particularly proud of it, SO ARE YOU ALL. You ask my business here. It seems to be the same as yours—to hold possession of this house! With this difference, however," he continued, taking a document from his pocket. "Here is the certificate, signed by the County Clerk, of the bill of sale of the entire Sisters' title to ME. It includes the whole two leagues from Fair Plains to the old boundary line of this rancho, which you forcibly entered this morning. There is the document; examine it if you like. The only shadow of a claim you could have to this property you would have to derive from ME. The only excuse you could have for this act of lawlessness would be orders from ME. And all that you have done this morning is only the assertion of MY legal right to this house. If I disavow your act, as I might, I leave you as helpless as any tramp that was ever kicked from a doorstep—as any burglar that was ever collared on the fence by a constable."

It was the truth. There was no denying the authority of the document, the facts of the situation, or its ultimate power and significance. There was consternation, stupefaction, and even a half-humorous recognition of the absurdity of their position on most of the faces around him. Incongruous as the scene was, it was made still more grotesque by the attitude of Jim Hooker. Ruthlessly abandoning the party of convicted trespassers, he stalked gloomily over to the side of Clarence, with the air of having been all the time scornfully in the secret and a mien of wearied victoriousness, and thus halting, he disdainfully expectorated tobacco juice on the ground between him and his late companions, as if to form a line of demarcation. The few Mexicans began to edge towards the gateway. This defection of his followers recalled the leader, who was no coward, to himself again.

"Shut the gate, there!" he shouted.

As its two sides clashed together again, he turned deliberately to Clarence.

Bret Harte

"That's all very well, young man, as regards the TITLE. You may have BOUGHT up the land, and legally own every square inch of howling wilderness between this and San Francisco, and I wish you joy of your d—d fool's bargain; you may have got a whole circus like that," pointing to the gloomy Jim, "at your back. But with all your money and all your friends you've forgotten one thing. You haven't got possession, and we have."

"That's just where we differ," said Clarence coolly, "for if you take the trouble to examine the house, you will see that it is already in possession of Mrs. Peyton—MY TENANT."

He paused to give effect to his revelations. But he was, nevertheless, unprepared for an unrehearsed dramatic situation. Mrs. Peyton, who had been tired of waiting, and was listening in the passage, at the mention of her name, entered the gallery, followed by the young ladies. The slight look of surprise upon her face at the revelation she had just heard of Clarence's ownership, only gave the suggestion of her having been unexpectedly disturbed in her peaceful seclusion. One of the Mexicans turned pale, with a frightened glance at the passage, as if he expected the figure of the dead man to follow.

The group fell back. The game was over—and lost. No one recognized it more quickly than the gamblers themselves. More than that, desperate and lawless as they were, they still retained the chivalry of Western men, and every hat was slowly doffed to the three black figures that stood silently in the gallery. And even apologetic speech began to loosen the clenched teeth of the discomfited leader.

"We—were—told there was no one in the house," he stammered.

"And it was the truth," said a pert, youthful, yet slightly affected voice. "For we climbed into the window just as you came in at the gate."

It was Susy's words that stung their ears again; but it was Susy's pretty figure, suddenly advanced and in a slightly theatrical attitude, that checked their anger. There had been a sudden ominous silence, as the whole plot of rescue seemed to be revealed to them in those audacious words. But a sense of the ludicrous, which too often was the only perception that ever mitigated the passions of such assemblies, here suddenly asserted itself. The leader burst into a loud laugh, which was echoed by the others, and, with waving hats, the whole party swept peacefully out through the gate.

"But what does all this mean about YOUR purchasing the land, Mr. Brant?" said Mrs. Peyton quickly, fixing her eyes intently on Clarence.

A faint color—the useless protest of his truthful blood—came to his cheek.

"The house is YOURS, and yours alone, Mrs. Peyton. The purchase of the sisters' title was a private arrangement between Mr. Peyton and myself, in view of an emergency like this."

She did not, however, take her proud, searching eyes from his face, and he was forced to turn away.

"It was SO like dear, good, thoughtful papa," said Susy. "Why, bless me," in a lower voice, "if that isn't that lying old Jim Hooker standing there by the gate!"

CHAPTER VIII

Judge Peyton had bequeathed his entire property uncondi-
tionally to his wife. But his affairs were found to be greatly
in disorder, and his papers in confusion, and although Mrs.
Peyton could discover no actual record of the late transaction
with Mr. Brant, which had saved her the possession of the
homestead, it was evident that he had spent large sums in
speculative attempts to maintain the integrity of his estate.
That enormous domain, although perfectly unencumbered,
had been nevertheless unremunerative, partly through the
costs of litigation and partly through the systematic depre-
dations to which its great size and long line of unprotected
boundary had subjected it. It had been invaded by squatters
and "jumpers," who had sown and reaped crops without
discovery; its cattle and wild horses had strayed or been
driven beyond its ill-defined and hopeless limits. Against
these difficulties the widow felt herself unable and unwilling
to contend, and with the advice of her friends and her lawyer,
she concluded to sell the estate, except that portion covered
by the Sisters' title, which, with the homestead, had been
reconveyed to her by Clarence. She retired with Susy to the
house in San Francisco, leaving Clarence to occupy and hold
the casa, with her servants, for her until order was restored.
The Robles Rancho thus became the headquarters of the new
owner of the Sisters' title, from which he administered its
affairs, visited its incumbencies, overlooked and surveyed its

lands, and—occasionally—collected its rents. There were not wanting critics who averred that these were scarcely remunerative, and that the young San Francisco fine gentleman, who was only Hamilton Brant's son, after all, yet who wished to ape the dignity and degree of a large landholder, had made a very foolish bargain. I grieve to say that one of his own tenants, namely, Jim Hooker, in his secret heart inclined to that belief, and looked upon Clarence's speculation as an act of far-seeing and inordinate vanity.

Indeed, the belligerent Jim had partly—and of course darkly —intimated something of this to Susy in their brief reunion at the casa during the few days that followed its successful reoccupation. And Clarence, remembering her older caprices, and her remark on her first recognition of him, was quite surprised at the easy familiarity of her reception of this forgotten companion of their childhood. But he was still more concerned in noticing, for the first time, a singular sympathetic understanding of each other, and an odd similarity of occasional action and expression between them. It was a part of this monstrous peculiarity that neither the sympathy nor the likeness suggested any particular friend-ship or amity in the pair, but rather a mutual antagonism and suspicion. Mrs. Peyton, coldly polite to Clarence's former COMPANION, but condescendingly gracious to his present TENANT and retainer, did not notice it, preoccupied with the annoyance and pain of Susy's frequent references to the old days of their democratic equality.

"You don't remember, Jim, the time that you painted my face in the wagon, and got me up as an Indian papoose?" she said mischievously.

But Jim, who had no desire to recall his previous humble position before Mrs. Peyton or Clarence, was only vaguely responsive. Clarence, although joyfully touched at this seeming evidence of Susy's loyalty to the past, nevertheless found himself even more acutely pained at the distress it caused Mrs. Peyton, and was as relieved as she was by Hooker's reticence. For he had seen little of Susy since Peyton's death, and there had been no repetition of their secret interviews. Neither had he, nor she as far as he could judge, noticed the omission. He had been more than usually kind, gentle, and protecting in his manner towards her, with little reference, however, to any response from her, yet he was vaguely conscious of some change in his feelings. He attributed it, when he thought of it at all, to the exciting experiences through which he had passed; to some sentiment of responsibility to his dead friend; and to another secret preoccupation that was always in his mind. He believed it would pass in time. Yet he felt a certain satisfaction that she was no longer able to trouble him, except, of course, when she pained Mrs. Peyton, and then he was half conscious of taking the old attitude of the dead husband in mediating between them. Yet so great was his inexperience that he believed, with pathetic simplicity of perception, that all this was due to the slow maturing of his love for her, and that he was still able to make her happy. But this was something to be thought of later. Just now Providence seemed to have offered him a vocation and a purpose that his idle adolescence had never known. He did not dream that his capacity for patience was only the slow wasting of his love.

Meantime that more wonderful change and recreation of the Californian landscape, so familiar, yet always so young, had come to the rancho. The league-long terrace that had yellowed, whitened, and wasted for half a year beneath a staring, monotonous sky, now under sailing clouds, flying and broken shafts of light, and sharply defined lines of rain, had taken a faint hue of resurrection. The dust that had muffled the roads and byways, and choked the low oaks that fringed the sunken canada, had long since been laid. The warm, moist breath of the southwest trades had softened the hard, dry lines of the landscape, and restored its color as of a picture over which a damp sponge had been passed. The broad expanse of plateau before the casa glistened and grew dark. The hidden woods of the canada, cleared and strengthened in their solitude, dripped along the trails and hollows that were now transformed into running streams. The distinguishing madrono near the entrance to the rancho had changed its crimson summer suit and masqueraded in buff and green.

Yet there were leaden days, when half the prospect seemed to be seen through palisades of rain; when the slight incline between the terraces became a tumultuous cascade, and the surest hoofs slipped on trails of unctuous mud; when cattle were bogged a few yards from the highway, and the crossing of the turnpike road was a dangerous ford. There were days of gale and tempest, when the shriveled stalks of giant oats were stricken like trees, and lay across each other in rigid angles, and a roar as of the sea came up from the writhing treetops in the sunken valley. There were long weary nights of steady downpour, hammering on the red tiles of the casa, and drumming on the shingles of the new veranda, which was more terrible to be borne. Alone, but for the servants, and an occasional storm-stayed tenant from Fair Plains, Clarence might have, at such times, questioned the effect of this seclusion upon his impassioned nature. But he had already been accustomed to monastic seclusion in his boyish life at El Refugio, and he did not reflect that, for that very reason, its indulgences might have been dangerous. From time to time letters reached him from the outer world of San Francisco—a few pleasant lines from Mrs. Peyton, in answer to his own chronicle of his half stewardship, giving the news of the family, and briefly recounting their movements. She was afraid that Susy's sensitive nature chafed under the restriction of mourning in the gay city, but she trusted to bring her back for a change to Robles when the rains were over. This was a poor substitute for those brief, happy glimpses of the home circle which had so charmed him, but he accepted it stoically. He wandered over the old house, from which the perfume of domesticity seemed to have evaporated, yet, notwithstanding Mrs. Peyton's playful permission, he never intruded upon the sanctity of the boudoir, and kept it jealously locked.

He was sitting in Peyton's business room one morning, when Incarnacion entered. Clarence had taken a fancy to this Indian, half steward, half vacquero, who had reciprocated it with a certain dog-like fidelity, but also a feline indirectness that was part of his nature. He had been early prepossessed with Clarence through a kinsman at El Refugio, where the young American's generosity had left a romantic record among the common people. He had been pleased to approve of his follies before the knowledge of his profitless and lordly land purchase had commended itself to him as corroborative testimony. "Of true hidalgo blood, mark you," he had said oracularly. "Wherefore was his father sacrificed by mongrels! As to the others, believe me—bah!"

He stood there, sombrero in hand, murky and confidential, steaming through his soaked serape and exhaling a blended odor of equine perspiration and cigarette smoke.

"It was, perhaps, as the master had noticed, a brigand's own day! Bullying, treacherous, and wicked! It blew you off your horse if you so much as lifted your arms and let the wind get inside your serape; and as for the mud—caramba! in fifty varas your forelegs were like bears, and your hoofs were earthen plasters!"

Clarence knew that Incarnacion had not sought him with

mere meteorological information, and patiently awaited further developments. The vacquero went on:—

"But one of the things this beast of a weather did was to wash down the stalks of the grain, and to clear out the trough and hollows between, and to make level the fields, and—look you! to uncover the stones and rubbish and whatever the summer dust had buried. Indeed, it was even as a miracle that Jose Mendez one day, after the first showers, came upon a silver button from his calzas, which he had lost in the early summer. And it was only that morning that, remembering how much and with what fire Don Clarencio had sought the missing boot from the foot of the Senor Peyton when his body was found, he, Incarnacion, had thought he would look for it on the falda of the second terrace. And behold, Mother of God it was there! Soaked with mud and rain, but the same as when the senor was alive. To the very spur!"

He drew the boot from beneath his serape and laid it before Clarence. The young man instantly recognized it, in spite of its weather-beaten condition and its air of grotesque and drunken inconsistency to the usually trim and correct appearance of Peyton when alive. "It is the same," he said, in a low voice.

"Good!" said Incarnacion. "Now, if Don Clarencio will examine the American spur, he will see—what? A few horse-hairs twisted and caught in the sharp points of the rowel. Good! Is it the hair of the horse that Senor rode? Clearly not; and in truth not. It is too long for the flanks and belly of the horse; it is not the same color as the tail and the mane. How comes it there? It comes from the twisted horsehair rope of a riata, and not from the braided cowhide thongs of the regular lasso of a vacquero. The lasso slips not much, but holds; the riata slips much and strangles."

Bret Harte

"But Mr. Peyton was not strangled," said Clarence quickly.

"No, for the noose of the riata was perhaps large—who knows? It might have slipped down his arms, pinioned him, and pulled him off. Truly!—such has been known before. Then on the ground it slipped again, or he perhaps worked it off to his feet where it caught on his spur, and then he was dragged until the boot came off, and behold! he was dead."

This had been Clarence's own theory of the murder, but he had only half confided it to Incarnacion. He silently examined the spur with the accusing horse-hair, and placed it in his desk. Incarnacion continued:—

"There is not a vacquero in the whole rancho who has a horse-hair riata. We use the braided cowhide; it is heavier and stronger; it is for the bull and not the man. The horse-hair riata comes from over the range—south."

There was a dead silence, broken only by the drumming of the rain upon the roof of the veranda. Incarnacion slightly shrugged his shoulders.

"Don Clarencio does not know the southern county? Francisco Robles, cousin of the 'Sisters,'—he they call 'Pancho,'—comes from the south. Surely when Don Clarencio bought the title he saw Francisco, for he was the steward?"

"I dealt only with the actual owners and through my bankers in San Francisco," returned Clarence abstractedly.

Incarnacion looked through the yellow corners of his murky eyes at his master.

"Pedro Valdez, who was sent away by Senor Peyton, is the

foster-brother of Francisco. They were much together. Now that Francisco is rich from the gold Don Clarencio paid for the title, they come not much together. But Pedro is rich, too. Mother of God! He gambles and is a fine gentleman. He holds his head high—even over the Americanos he gambles with. Truly, they say he can shoot with the best of them. He boasts and swells himself, this Pedro! He says if all the old families were like him, they would drive those western swine back over the mountains again."

Clarence raised his eyes, caught a subtle yellow flash from Incarnacion's, gazed at him suddenly, and rose.

"I don't think I have ever seen him," he said quietly. "Thank you for bringing me the spur. But keep the knowledge of it to yourself, good Nascio, for the present."

Nascio nevertheless still lingered. Perceiving which, Clarence handed him a cigarette and proceeded to light one himself. He knew that the vacquero would reroll his, and that that always deliberate occupation would cover and be an excuse for further confidence.

"The Senora Peyton does not perhaps meet this Pedro in the society of San Francisco?"

"Surely not. The senora is in mourning and goes not out in society, nor would she probably go anywhere where she would meet a dismissed servant of her husband."

Incarnacion slowly lit his cigarette, and said between the puffs, "And the senorita—she would not meet him?"

"Assuredly not."

"And," continued Incarnacion, throwing down the match and

putting his foot on it, "if this boaster, this turkey-cock, says she did, you could put him out like that?"

"Certainly," said Clarence, with an easy confidence he was, however, far from feeling, "if he really SAID it—which I doubt."

"Ah, truly," said Incarnacion; "who knows? It may be another Senorita Silsbee."

"The senora's adopted daughter is called MISS PEYTON, friend Nascio. You forget yourself," said Clarence quietly.

"Ah, pardon!" said Incarnacion with effusive apology; "but she was born Silsbee. Everybody knows it; she herself has told it to Pepita. The Senor Peyton bequeathed his estate to the Senora Peyton. He named not the senorita! Eh, what would you? It is the common cackle of the barnyard. But I say 'Mees Silsbee.' For look you. There is a Silsbee of Sacramento, the daughter of her aunt, who writes letters to her. Pepita has seen them! And possibly it is only that Mees of whom the brigand Pedro boasts."

"Possibly," said Clarence, "but as far as this rancho is concerned, friend Nascio, thou wilt understand—and I look to thee to make the others understand—that there is no Senorita SILSBEE here, only the Senorita PEYTON, the respected daughter of the senora thy mistress!" He spoke with the quaint mingling of familiarity and paternal gravity of the Spanish master—a faculty he had acquired at El Refugio in a like vicarious position, and which never failed as a sign of authority. "And now," he added gravely, "get out of this, friend, with God's blessing, and see that thou rememberest what I told thee."

The retainer, with equal gravity, stepped backwards, saluted with his sombrero until the stiff brim scraped the floor, and then solemnly withdrew.

Left to himself, Clarence remained for an instant silent and thoughtful before the oven-like hearth. So! everybody knew Susy's real relations to the Peytons, and everybody but Mrs. Peyton, perhaps, knew that she was secretly corresponding with some one of her own family. In other circumstances he might have found some excuse for this assertion of her independence and love of her kindred, but in her attitude towards Mrs. Peyton it seemed monstrous. It appeared impossible that Mrs. Peyton should not have heard of it, or suspected the young girl's disaffection. Perhaps she had—it was another burden laid upon her shoulders—but the proud woman had kept it to herself. A film of moisture came across his eyes. I fear he thought less of the suggestion of Susy's secret meeting with Pedro, or Incarnacion's implied suspicions that Pedro was concerned in Peyton's death, than of this sentimental possibility. He knew that Pedro had been hated by the others on account of his position; he knew the instinctive jealousies of the race and their predisposition to extravagant misconstruction. From what he had gathered, and particularly from the voices he had overheard on the Fair Plains Road, it seemed to him that Pedro was more capable of mercenary intrigue than physical revenge. He was not aware of the irrevocable affront put upon Pedro by Peyton, and he had consequently attached no importance to Peyton's own half-scornful intimation of the only kind of retaliation that Pedro would be likely to take. The unsuccessful attempt upon himself he had always thought might have been an accident, or if it was really a premeditated assault, it might have been intended actually for HIMSELF and not Peyton, as he had first thought, and his old friend had suffered for HIM, through some mistake of the assailant. The purpose, which alone seemed wanting, might have been to remove Clarence as a possible witness who had overheard their

Bret Harte

conspiracy—how much of it they did not know—on the Fair Plains Road that night. The only clue he held to the murderer in the spur locked in his desk, merely led him beyond the confines of the rancho, but definitely nowhere else. It was, however, some relief to know that the crime was not committed by one of Peyton's retainers, nor the outcome of domestic treachery.

After some consideration he resolved to seek Jim Hooker, who might be possessed of some information respecting Susy's relations, either from the young girl's own confidences or from Jim's personal knowledge of the old frontier families. From a sense of loyalty to Susy and Mrs. Peyton, he had never alluded to the subject before him, but since the young girl's own indiscretion had made it a matter of common report, however distasteful it was to his own feelings, he felt he could not plead the sense of delicacy for her. He had great hopes in what he had always believed was only her exaggeration of fact as well as feeling. And he had an instinctive reliance on her fellow poseur's ability to detect it. A few days later, when he found he could safely leave the rancho alone, he rode to Fair Plains.

The floods were out along the turnpike road, and even seemed to have increased since his last journey. The face of the landscape had changed again. One of the lower terraces had become a wild mere of sedge and reeds. The dry and dusty bed of a forgotten brook had reappeared, a full-banked river, crossing the turnpike and compelling a long detour before the traveler could ford it. But as he approached the Hopkins farm and the opposite clearing and cabin of Jim Hooker, he was quite unprepared for a still more remarkable transformation. The cabin, a three-roomed structure, and its cattle-shed had entirely disappeared! There were no traces or signs of inundation. The land lay on a gentle acclivity above the farm and secure from the effects of the flood, and a part of the ploughed and cleared land around the site of the cabin showed no evidence of overflow on its black, upturned soil. But the house was gone! Only a few timbers too heavy to be removed, the blighting erasions of a few months of occupation, and the dull, blackened area of the site itself were to be seen. The fence alone was intact.

Clarence halted before it, perplexed and astonished. Scarcely two weeks had elapsed since he had last visited it and sat beneath its roof with Jim, and already its few ruins had taken upon themselves the look of years of abandonment and decay. The wild land seemed to have thrown off its yoke of cultivation in a night, and nature rioted again with all its primal forces over the freed soil. Wild oats and mustard were springing already in the broken furrows, and lank vines were slimily spreading over a few scattered but still unseasoned and sappy shingles. Some battered tin cans and fragments of old clothing looked as remote as if they had been relics of the earliest immigration.

Clarence turned inquiringly towards the Hopkins farmhouse across the road. His arrival, however, had already been noticed, as the door of the kitchen opened in an anticipatory fashion, and he could see the slight figure of Phoebe Hopkins in the doorway, backed by the overlooking heads and shoulders of her parents. The face of the young girl was pale and drawn with anxiety, at which Clarence's simple astonishment took a shade of concern.

"I am looking for Mr. Hooker," he said uneasily. "And I don't seem to be able to find either him or his house."

"And you don't know what's gone of him?" said the girl quickly.

"No; I haven't seen him for two weeks."

114   Bret Harte

"There, I told you so!" said the girl, turning nervously to her parents. "I knew it. He hasn't seen him for two weeks." Then, looking almost tearfully at Clarence's face, she said, "No more have we."

"But," said Clarence impatiently, "something must have happened. Where is his house?"

"Taken away by them jumpers," interrupted the old farmer; "a lot of roughs that pulled it down and carted it off in a jiffy before our very eyes without answerin' a civil question to me or her. But he wasn't there, nor before, nor since."

"No," added the old woman, with flashing eyes, "or he'd let 'em have what ther' was in his six-shooters."

"No, he wouldn't, mother," said the girl impatiently, "he'd CHANGED, and was agin all them ideas of force and riotin'. He was for peace and law all the time. Why, the day before we missed him he was tellin' me California never would be decent until people obeyed the laws and the titles were settled. And for that reason, because he wouldn't fight agin the law, or without the consent of the law, they've killed him, or kidnapped him away."

The girl's lips quivered, and her small brown hands twisted the edges of her blue checked apron. Although this new picture of Jim's peacefulness was as astounding and unsatisfactory as his own disappearance, there was no doubt of the sincerity of poor Phoebe's impression.

In vain did Clarence point out to them there must be some mistake; that the trespassers—the so-called jumpers—really belonged to the same party as Hooker, and would have no reason to dispossess him; that, in fact, they were all HIS, Clarence's, tenants. In vain he assured them of Hooker's perfect security in possession; that he could have driven the intruders away by the simple exhibition of his lease, or that he could have even called a constable from the town of Fair Plains to protect him from mere lawlessness. In vain did he assure them of his intention to find his missing friend, and reinstate him at any cost. The conviction that the unfortunate young man had been foully dealt with was fixed in the minds of the two women. For a moment Clarence himself was staggered by it.

"You see," said the young girl, with a kindling face, "the day before he came back from Robles, ther' were some queer men hangin' round his cabin, but as they were the same kind that went off with him the day the Sisters' title was confirmed, we thought nothing of it. But when he came back from you he seemed worried and anxious, and wasn't a bit like himself. We thought perhaps he'd got into some trouble there, or been disappointed. He hadn't, had he, Mr. Brant?" continued Phoebe, with an appealing look.

"By no means," said Clarence warmly. "On the contrary, he was able to do his friends good service there, and was successful in what he attempted. Mrs. Peyton was very grateful. Of course he told you what had happened, and what he did for us," continued Clarence, with a smile.

He had already amused himself on the way with a fanciful conception of the exaggerated account Jim had given of his exploits. But the bewildered girl shook her head.

"No, he didn't tell us ANYTHING."

Clarence was really alarmed. This unprecedented abstention of Hooker's was portentous.

"He didn't say anything but what I told you about law and

order," she went on; "but that same night we heard a good deal of talking and shouting in the cabin and around it. And the next day he was talking with father, and wanting to know how HE kept his land without trouble from outsiders."

"And I said," broke in Hopkins, "that I guessed folks didn't bother a man with women folks around, and that I kalkilated that I wasn't quite as notorious for fightin' as he was."

"And he said," also interrupted Mrs. Hopkins, "and quite in his nat'ral way, too—gloomy like, you remember, Cyrus," appealingly to her husband—"that that was his curse."

The smile that flickered around Clarence's mouth faded, however, as he caught sight of Phoebe's pleading, interrogating eyes. It was really too bad. Whatever change had come over the rascal it was too evident that his previous belligerent personality had had its full effect upon the simple girl, and that, hereafter, one pair of honest eyes would be wistfully following him.

Perplexed and indignant, Clarence again closely questioned her as to the personnel of the trespassing party who had been seen once or twice since passing over the field. He had at last elicited enough information to identify one of them as Gilroy, the leader of the party that had invaded Robles rancho. His cheek flushed. Even if they had wished to take a theatrical and momentary revenge on Hooker for the passing treachery to them which they had just discovered, although such retaliation was only transitory, and they could not hold the land, it was an insult to Clarence himself, whose tenant Jim was, and subversive of all their legally acquired rights. He would confront this Gilroy at once; his half-wild encampment was only a few miles away, just over the boundaries of the Robles estate. Without stating his intention, he took leave of the Hopkins family with the cheerful assurance that he would probably return with some news of Hooker, and rode away.

The trail became more indistinct and unfrequented as it diverged from the main road, and presently lost itself in the slope towards the east. The horizon grew larger: there were faint bluish lines upon it which he knew were distant mountains; beyond this a still fainter white line—the Sierran snows. Presently he intersected a trail running south, and remarked that it crossed the highway behind him, where he had once met the two mysterious horsemen. They had evidently reached the terrace through the wild oats by that trail. A little farther on were a few groups of sheds and canvas tents in a bare and open space, with scattered cattle and horsemen, exactly like an encampment, or the gathering of a country fair. As Clarence rode down towards them he could see that his approach was instantly observed, and that a simultaneous movement was made as if to anticipate him. For the first time he realized the possible consequences of his visit, single-handed, but it was too late to retrace his steps. With a glance at his holster, he rode boldly forward to the nearest shed. A dozen men hovered near him, but something in his quiet, determined manner held them aloof. Gilroy was on the threshold in his shirtsleeves. A single look showed him that Clarence was alone, and with a careless gesture of his hand he warned away his own followers.

"You've got a sort of easy way of droppin' in whar you ain't invited, Brant," he said with a grim smile, which was not, however, without a certain air of approval. "Got it from your father, didn't you?"

"I don't know, but I don't believe HE ever thought it necessary to warn twenty men of the approach of ONE," replied Clarence, in the same tone. "I had no time to stand on ceremony, for I have just come from Hooker's quarter section at Fair Plains."

Gilroy smiled again, and gazed abstractedly at the sky.

"You know as well as I do," said Clarence, controlling his voice with an effort, "that what you have done there will have to be undone, if you wish to hold even those lawless men of yours together, or keep yourself and them from being run into the brush like highwaymen. I've no fear for that. Neither do I care to know what was your motive in doing it; but I can only tell you that if it was retaliation, I alone was and still am responsible for Hooker's action at the rancho. I came here to know just what you have done with him, and, if necessary, to take his place."

"You're just a little too previous in your talk, I reckon, Brant," returned Gilroy lazily, "and as to legality, I reckon we stand on the same level with yourself, just here. Beginnin' with what you came for: as we don't know where your Jim Hooker is, and as we ain't done anythin' to HIM, we don't exackly see what we could do with YOU in his place. Ez to our motives—well, we've got a good deal to say about THAT. We reckoned that he wasn't exackly the kind of man we wanted for a neighbor. His pow'ful fightin' style didn't suit us peaceful folks, and we thought it rather worked agin this new 'law and order' racket to have such a man about, to say nuthin' of it prejudicin' quiet settlers. He had too many revolvers for one man to keep his eye on, and was altogether too much steeped in blood, so to speak, for ordinary washin' and domestic purposes! His hull get up was too deathlike and clammy; so we persuaded him to leave. We just went there, all of us, and exhorted him. We stayed round there two days and nights, takin' turns, talkin' with him, nuthin' more, only selecting subjects in his own style to please him, until he left! And then, as we didn't see any use for his house there, we took it away. Them's the cold facts, Brant," he added, with a certain convincing indifference that left no room for doubt, "and you can stand by 'em. Now, workin' back to the first principle you laid down—that we'll have to UNDO what we've DONE—we don't agree with you, for we've taken a leaf outer your own book. We've got it here in black and white. We've got a bill o' sale of Hooker's house and possession, and we're on the land in place of him—AS YOUR TENANTS." He reentered the shanty, took a piece of paper from a soap-box on the shell, and held it out to Clarence. "Here it is. It's a fair and square deal, Brant. We gave him, as it says here, a hundred dollars for it! No humbuggin', but the hard cash, by Jiminy! AND HE TOOK THE MONEY."

The ring of truth in the man's voice was as unmistakable as the signature in Jim's own hand. Hooker had sold out! Clarence turned hastily away.

"We don't know where he went," continued Gilroy grimly, "but I reckon you ain't over anxious to see him NOW. And I kin tell ye something to ease your mind—he didn't require much persuadin'. And I kin tell ye another, if ye ain't above takin' advice from folks that don't pertend to give it," he added, with the same curious look of interest in his face. "You've done well to get shut of him, and if you got shut of a few more of his kind that you trust to, you'd do better."

As if to avoid noticing any angry reply from the young man, he reentered the cabin and shut the door behind him. Clarence felt the uselessness of further parley, and rode away.

But Gilroy's Parthian arrow rankled as he rode. He was not greatly shocked at Jim's defection, for he was always fully conscious of his vanity and weakness; but he was by no means certain that Jim's extravagance and braggadocio, which he had found only amusing and, perhaps, even pathetic, might not be as provocative and prejudicial to others as Gilroy had said. But, like all sympathetic and unselfish natures, he sought to find some excuse for his old companion's weakness in his own mistaken judgment. He had no business to bring poor Jim on the land, to subject his singular temperament to the temptations of such a life and such surroundings; he should never have made use of his services at the rancho. He had done him harm rather than good in his ill-advised, and, perhaps, SELFISH attempts to help him. I have said that Gilroy's parting warning rankled in his breast, but not ignobly. It wounded the surface of his sensitive nature, but could not taint or corrupt the pure, wholesome blood of the gentleman beneath it. For in Gilroy's warning he saw only his own shortcomings. A strange fatality had marked his friendships. He had been no help to Jim; he had brought no happiness to Susy or Mrs. Peyton, whose disagreement his visit seemed to have accented. Thinking over the mysterious attack upon himself, it now seemed to him possible that, in some obscure way, his presence at the rancho had precipitated the more serious attack on Peyton. If, as it had been said, there was some curse upon his inheritance from his father, he seemed to have made others share it with him. He was riding onward abstractedly, with his head sunk on his breast and his eyes fixed upon some vague point between his horse's sensitive ears, when a sudden, intelligent, forward pricking of them startled him, and an apparition arose from the plain before him that seemed to sweep all other sense away.

It was the figure of a handsome young horseman as abstracted as himself, but evidently on better terms with his own personality. He was dark haired, sallow cheeked, and blue eyed—the type of the old Spanish Californian. A burnt-out cigarette was in his mouth, and he was riding a roan mustang with the lazy grace of his race. But what arrested

Clarence's attention more than his picturesque person was the narrow, flexible, long coil of gray horse-hair riata which hung from his saddle-bow, but whose knotted and silver-beaded terminating lash he was swirling idly in his narrow brown hand. Clarence knew and instantly recognized it as the ordinary fanciful appendage of a gentleman rider, used for tethering his horse on lonely plains, and always made the object of the most lavish expenditure of decoration and artistic skill. But he was as suddenly filled with a blind, unreasoning sense of repulsion and fury, and lifted his eyes to the man as he approached. What the stranger saw in Clarence's blazing eyes no one but himself knew, for his own became fixed and staring; his sallow cheeks grew lanker and livid; his careless, jaunty bearing stiffened into rigidity, and swerving his horse to one side he suddenly passed Clarence at a furious gallop. The young American wheeled quickly, and for an instant his knees convulsively gripped the flanks of his horse to follow. But the next moment he recalled himself, and with an effort began to collect his thoughts. What was he intending to do, and for what reason! He had met hundreds of such horsemen before, and caparisoned and accoutred like this, even to the riata. And he certainly was not dressed like either of the mysterious horsemen whom he had overheard that moonlight evening. He looked back; the stranger had already slackened his pace, and was slowly disappearing. Clarence turned and rode on his way.

CHAPTER IX

Without disclosing the full extent of Jim's defection and desertion, Clarence was able to truthfully assure the Hopkins family of his personal safety, and to promise that he would continue his quest, and send them further news of the absentee. He believed it would be found that Jim had been called away on some important business, but that not daring to leave his new shanty exposed and temptingly unprotected, he had made a virtue of necessity by selling it to his neighbors, intending to build a better house on its site after his return. Having comforted Phoebe, and impulsively conceived further plans for restoring Jim to her—happily without any recurrence of his previous doubts as to his own efficacy as a special Providence—he returned to the rancho. If he thought again of Jim's defection and Gilroy's warning, it was only to strengthen himself to a clearer perception of his unselfish duty and singleness of purpose. He would give up brooding, apply himself more practically to the management of the property, carry out his plans for the foundation of a Landlords' Protective League for the southern counties, become a candidate for the Legislature, and, in brief, try to fill Peyton's place in the county as he had at the rancho. He would endeavor to become better acquainted with the half-breed laborers on the estate and avoid the friction between them and the Americans; he was conscious that he had not made that use of his early familiarity with their ways and language which he might have done. If, occasionally, the figure of the young Spaniard whom he had met on the lonely road obtruded itself on him, it was always with the instinctive premonition that he would meet him again, and the mystery of the sudden repulsion be in some way explained. Thus Clarence! But the momentary impulse that had driven him to Fair Plains, the eagerness to set his mind at rest regarding Susy and her relatives, he had utterly forgotten.

Howbeit some of the energy and enthusiasm that he breathed into these various essays made their impression. He succeeded in forming the Landlords' League; under a commission suggested by him the straggling boundaries of Robles and the adjacent claims were resurveyed, defined, and mutually protected; even the lawless Gilroy, from extending an amused toleration to the young administrator, grew to recognize and accept him; the peons and vacqueros began to have faith in a man who acknowledged them sufficiently to rebuild the ruined Mission Chapel on the estate, and save them the long pilgrimage to Santa Inez on Sundays and saints' days; the San Francisco priest imported from Clarence's old college at San Jose, and an habitual guest at Clarence's hospitable board, was grateful enough to fill his flock with loyalty to the young padron.

He had returned from a long drive one afternoon, and had just thrown himself into an easy-chair with the comfortable consciousness of a rest fairly earned. The dull embers of a fire occasionally glowed in the oven-like hearth, although the open casement of a window let in the soft breath of the southwest trades. The angelus had just rung from the restored chapel, and, mellowed by distance, seemed to Clarence to lend that repose to the wind-swept landscape that it had always lacked.

Bret Harte

Suddenly his quick ear detected the sound of wheels in the ruts of the carriage way. Usually his visitors to the casa came on horseback, and carts and wagons used only the lower road. As the sound approached nearer, an odd fancy filled his heart with unaccountable pleasure. Could it be Mrs. Peyton making an unexpected visit to the rancho? He held his breath. The vehicle was now rolling on into the patio. The clatter of hoofs and a halt were followed by the accents of women's voices. One seemed familiar. He rose quickly, as light footsteps ran along the corridor, and then the door opened impetuously to the laughing face of Susy!

He came towards her hastily, yet with only the simple impulse of astonishment. He had no thought of kissing her, but as he approached, she threw her charming head archly to one side, with a mischievous knitting of her brows and a significant gesture towards the passage, that indicated the proximity of a stranger and the possibility of interruption.

"Hush! Mrs. McClosky's here," she whispered.

"Mrs. McClosky?" repeated Clarence vaguely.

"Yes, of course," impatiently. "My Aunt Jane. Silly! We just cut away down here to surprise you. Aunty's never seen the place, and here was a good chance."

"And your mother—Mrs. Peyton? Has she—does she?"—stammered Clarence.

"Has she—does she?" mimicked Susy, with increasing impatience. "Why, of course she DOESN'T know anything about it. She thinks I'm visiting Mary Rogers at Oakland. And I am—AFTERWARDS," she laughed. "I just wrote to Aunt Jane to meet me at Alameda, and we took the stage to Santa Inez and drove on here in a buggy. Wasn't it real fun?

Tell me, Clarence! You don't say anything! Tell me—wasn't it real fun?"

This was all so like her old, childlike, charming, irresponsible self, that Clarence, troubled and bewildered as he was, took her hands and drew her like a child towards him.

"Of course," she went on, yet stopping to smell a rosebud in his buttonhole, "I have a perfect right to come to my own home, goodness knows! and if I bring my own aunt, a married woman, with me—although," loftily, "there may be a young unmarried gentleman alone there—still I fail to see any impropriety in it!"

He was still holding her; but in that instant her manner had completely changed again; the old Susy seemed to have slipped away and evaded him, and he was retaining only a conscious actress in his arms.

"Release me, Mr. Brant, please," she said, with a languid affected glance behind her; "we are not alone."

Then, as the rustling of a skirt sounded nearer in the passage, she seemed to change back to her old self once more, and with a lightning flash of significance whispered—

"She knows everything!"

To add to Clarence's confusion, the woman who entered cast a quick glance of playful meaning on the separating youthful pair. She was an ineffective blonde with a certain beauty that seemed to be gradually succumbing to the ravages of paint and powder rather than years; her dress appeared to have suffered from an equally unwise excess of ornamentation and trimming, and she gave the general impression of having been intended for exhibition in almost any other light than the one in which she happened to be. There were two or three mud-stains on the laces of her sleeve and underskirt that were obtrusively incongruous. Her voice, which had, however, a ring of honest intention in it, was somewhat over-strained, and evidently had not yet adjusted itself to the low-ceilinged, conventual-like building.

"There, children, don't mind me! I know I'm not on in this scene, but I got nervous waiting there, in what you call the 'salon,' with only those Greaser servants staring round me in a circle, like a regular chorus. My! but it's anteek here—regular anteek—Spanish." Then, with a glance at Clarence, "So this is Clarence Brant—your Clarence? Interduce me, Susy."

In his confusion of indignation, pain, and even a certain conception of the grim ludicrousness of the situation, Clarence grasped despairingly at the single sentence of Susy's. "In my own home." Surely, at least, it was HER OWN HOME, and as he was only the business agent of her adopted mother, he had no right to dictate to her under what circumstances she should return to it, or whom she should introduce there. In her independence and caprice Susy might easily have gone elsewhere with this astounding relative, and would Mrs. Peyton like it better? Clinging to this idea, his instinct of hospitality asserted itself. He welcomed Mrs. McClosky with nervous effusion:—

"I am only Mrs. Peyton's major domo here, but any guest of her DAUGHTER'S is welcome."

"Yes," said Mrs. McClosky, with ostentatious archness, "I reckon Susy and I understand your position here, and you've got a good berth of it. But we won't trouble you much on Mrs. Peyton's account, will we, Susy? And now she and me will just take a look around the shanty—it is real old Spanish anteek, ain't it?—and sorter take stock of it, and you young folks will have to tear yourselves apart for a while, and play propriety before me. You've got to be on your good behavior while I'm here, I can tell you! I'm a heavy old 'doo-anna.' Ain't I, Susy? School-ma'ms and mother superiors ain't in the game with ME for discipline."

She threw her arms around the young girl's waist and drew her towards her affectionately, an action that slightly precipitated some powder upon the black dress of her niece. Susy glanced mischievously at Clarence, but withdrew her eyes presently to let them rest with unmistakable appreciation and admiration on her relative. A pang shot through Clarence's breast. He had never seen her look in that way at Mrs. Peyton. Yet here was this stranger, provincial, overdressed, and extravagant, whose vulgarity was only made tolerable through her good humor, who had awakened that interest which the refined Mrs. Peyton had never yet been able to touch. As Mrs. McClosky swept out of the room with Susy he turned away with a sinking heart.

Yet it was necessary that the Spanish house servants should not suspect this treason to their mistress, and Clarence stopped their childish curiosity about the stranger with a careless and easy acceptance of Susy's sudden visit in the light of an ordinary occurrence, and with a familiarity towards Mrs. McClosky which became the more distasteful to him in proportion as he saw that it was evidently agreeable to her. But, easily responsive, she became speedily confidential. Without a single question from himself, or a contributing remark from Susy, in half an hour she had told him her whole history. How, as Jane Silsbee, an elder sister of Susy's mother, she had early eloped from the paternal home in Kansas with McClosky, a strolling actor. How she had married him and gone on the stage under his stage name, effectively preventing any recognition by her family. How, coming to California, where her husband had become manager of the theatre at Sacramento, she was indignant to find that her only surviving relation, a sister-in-law, living in the same place, had for a money consideration given up all claim to the orphaned Susy, and how she had resolved to find out "if the poor child was happy." How she succeeded in finding out that she was not happy. How she wrote to her, and even met her secretly at San Francisco and Oakland, and how she had undertaken this journey partly for "a lark," and partly to see Clarence and the property. There was no doubt of the speaker's sincerity; with this outrageous candor there was an equal obliviousness of any indelicacy in her conduct towards Mrs. Peyton that seemed hopeless. Yet he must talk plainly to her; he must say to her what he could not say to Susy; upon HER Mrs. Peyton's happiness—he believed he was thinking of Susy's also—depended. He must take the first opportunity of speaking to her alone.

That opportunity came sooner than he had expected. After dinner, Mrs. McClosky turned to Susy, and playfully telling her that she had "to talk business" with Mr. Brant, bade her go to the salon and await her. When the young girl left the room, she looked at Clarence, and, with that assumption of curtness with which coarse but kindly natures believe they overcome the difficulty of delicate subjects, said abruptly:—

"Well, young man, now what's all this between you and Susy? I'm looking after her interests—same as if she was my own girl. If you've got anything to say, now's your time. And don't you shilly-shally too long over it, either, for you might as well know that a girl like that can have her pick and choice, and be beholden to no one; and when she don't care to choose, there's me and my husband ready to do for her all the same. We mightn't be able to do the anteek Spanish Squire, but we've got our own line of business, and it's a comfortable one."

To have this said to him under the roof of Mrs. Peyton, from whom, in his sensitiveness, he had thus far jealously guarded his own secret, was even more than Clarence's gentleness could stand, and fixed his wavering resolution.

"I don't think we quite understand each other, Mrs. McClosky," he said coldly, but with glittering eyes. "I have certainly something to say to you; if it is not on a subject as pleasant as the one you propose, it is, nevertheless, one that I think you and I are more competent to discuss together."

Then, with quiet but unrelenting directness, he pointed out to her that Susy was a legally adopted daughter of Mrs. Peyton, and, as a minor, utterly under her control; that Mrs. Peyton had no knowledge of any opposing relatives; and that Susy had not only concealed the fact from her, but that he was satisfied that Mrs. Peyton did not even know of Susy's discontent and alienation; that she had tenderly and carefully brought up the helpless orphan as her own child, and even if she had not gained her affection was at least entitled to her obedience and respect; that while Susy's girlish caprice and inexperience excused HER conduct, Mrs. Peyton and her friends would have a right to expect more consideration from a person of Mrs. McClosky's maturer judgment. That for these reasons, and as the friend of Mrs. Peyton, whom he could alone recognize as Susy's guardian and the arbiter of her affections, he must decline to discuss the young girl with any reference to himself or his own intentions.

An unmistakable flush asserted itself under the lady's powder.

"Suit yourself, young man, suit yourself," she said, with equally direct resentment and antagonism; "only mebbee you'll let me tell you that Jim McClosky ain't no fool, and mebbee knows what lawyers think of an arrangement with a sister-in-law that leaves a real sister out! Mebbee that's a 'Sister's title' you ain't thought of, Mr. Brant! And mebbee you'll find out that your chance o' gettin' Mrs. Peyton's consent ain't as safe to gamble on as you reckon it is. And mebbee, what's more to the purpose, if you DID get it, it might not be just the trump card to fetch Susy with! And to wind up, Mr. Brant, when you DO have to come down to the bed-rock and me and Jim McClosky, you may find out that him and me have discovered a better match for Susy than the son of old Ham Brant, who is trying to play the Spanish grandee off his father's money on a couple of women. And we mayn't have to go far to do it—or to get THE REAL THING, Mr. Brant!"

Too heartsick and disgusted to even notice the slur upon himself or the import of her last words, Clarence only rose and bowed as she jumped up from the table. But as she reached the door he said, half appealingly:—

"Whatever are your other intentions, Mrs. McClosky, as we are both Susy's guests, I beg you will say nothing of this to her while we are here, and particularly that you will not allow her to think for a moment that I have discussed MY relations to her with anybody."

She flung herself out of the door without a reply; but on entering the dark low-ceilinged drawing-room she was surprised to find that Susy was not there. She was conesquently obliged to return to the veranda, where Clarence had withdrawn, and to somewhat ostentatiously demand of the servants that Susy should be sent to her room at once. But the young girl was not in her own room, and was apparently nowhere to be found. Clarence, who had now fully determined as a last resource to make a direct appeal to Susy herself, listened to this fruitless search with some concern. She could not have gone out in the rain, which was again falling. She might be hiding somewhere to avoid a recurrence of the scene she had perhaps partly overheard. He turned into the corridor that led to Mrs. Peyton's boudoir. As he knew that it was locked, he was surprised to see by the dim light of the hanging lamp that a duplicate key to the one in his desk was in the lock. It must be Susy's, and the young girl had probably taken refuge there. He knocked gently. There was a rustle in the room and the sound of a chair being moved, but no reply. Impelled by a sudden instinct he opened the door, and was met by a cool current of air from some open window. At the same moment the figure of Susy approached him from the semi-darkness of the interior.

"I did not know you were here," said Clarence, much relieved, he knew not why, "but I am glad, for I wanted to speak with you alone for a few moments."

She did not reply, but he drew a match from his pocket and lit the two candles which he knew stood on the table. The wick of one was still warm, as if it had been recently extinguished. As the light slowly radiated, he could see that she was regarding him with an air of affected unconcern, but a somewhat heightened color. It was like her, and not inconsistent with his idea that she had come there to avoid an after scene with Mrs. McClosky or himself, or perhaps both. The room was not disarranged in any way. The window that was opened was the casement of the deep embrasured one in the rear wall, and the light curtain before it still swayed occasionally in the night wind.

"I'm afraid I had a row with your aunt, Susy," he began lightly, in his old familiar way; "but I had to tell her I didn't think her conduct to Mrs. Peyton was exactly the square thing towards one who had been as devoted to you as she has been."

"Oh, for goodness' sake, don't go over all that again," said Susy impatiently. "I've had enough of it."

Clarence flashed, but recovered himself.

"Then you overheard what I said, and know what I think," he said calmly.

"I knew it BEFORE," said the young girl, with a slight supercilious toss of the head, and yet a certain abstraction of manner as she went to the window and closed it. "Anybody could see it! I know you always wanted me to stay here with Mrs. Peyton, and be coddled and monitored and catechised and shut up away from any one, until YOU had been coddled and monitored and catechised by somebody else sufficiently to suit her ideas of your being a fit husband for me. I told aunty it was no use our coming here to—to"—

"To do what?" asked Clarence.

"To put some spirit into you," said the young girl, turning upon him sharply; "to keep you from being tied to that woman's apron-strings. To keep her from making a slave of you as she would of me. But it is of no use. Mary Rogers was right when she said you had no wish to please anybody but Mrs. Peyton, and no eyes for anybody but her. And if it hadn't been too ridiculous, considering her age and yours, she'd say you were dead in love with her."

For an instant Clarence felt the blood rush to his face and then sink away, leaving him pale and cold. The room, which had seemed to whirl around him, and then fade away, returned with appalling distinctness—the distinctness of memory—and a vision of the first day that he had seen Mrs. Peyton sitting there, as he seemed to see her now. For the first time there flashed upon him the conviction that the young girl had spoken the truth, and had brusquely brushed the veil from his foolish eyes. He WAS in love with Mrs. Peyton! That was what his doubts and hesitation regarding Susy meant. That alone was the source, secret, and limit of his vague ambition.

But with the conviction came a singular calm. In the last few moments he seemed to have grown older, to have loosed the bonds of old companionship with Susy, and the later impresssion she had given him of her mature knowledge, and moved on far beyond her years and experience. And it was with an authority that was half paternal, and in a voice he himself scarcely recognized, that he said:—

"If I did not know you were prejudiced by a foolish and indiscreet woman, I should believe that you were trying to insult me as you have your adopted mother, and would save you the pain of doing both in HER house by leaving it now and forever. But because I believe you are controlled against your best instinct by that woman, I shall remain here with you to frustrate her as best I can, or until I am able to lay everything before Mrs. Peyton except the foolish speech you have just made."

The young girl laughed. "Why not THAT one too, while you're about it? See what she'll say."

"I shall tell her," continued Clarence calmly, "only what YOU yourself have made it necessary for me to tell her to save you from folly and disgrace, and only enough to spare her the mortification of hearing it first from her own servants."

"Hearing WHAT from her own servants? What do you mean? How dare you?" demanded the young girl sharply.

She was quite real in her anxiety now, although her attitude of virtuous indignation struck him as being like all her emotional expression, namely, acting.

"I mean that the servants know of your correspondence with Mrs. McClosky, and that she claims to be your aunt," returned Clarence. "They know that you confided to Pepita. They believe that either Mrs. McClosky or you have seen"—

He had stopped suddenly. He was about to say that the servants (particularly Incarnacion) knew that Pedro had boasted of having met Susy, when, for the first time, the tremendous significance of what he had hitherto considered as merely an idle falsehood flashed upon him.

"Seen whom?" repeated Susy in a higher voice, impatiently stamping her foot.

Clarence looked at her, and in her excited, questioning face saw a confirmation of his still half-formed suspicions. In his own abrupt pause and knitted eyebrows she must have read his thoughts also. Their eyes met. Her violet pupils dilated, trembled, and then quickly shifted as she suddenly stiffened into an attitude of scornful indifference, almost grotesque in its unreality. His eyes slowly turned to the window, the door, the candles on the table and the chair before it, and then came back to her face again. Then he drew a deep breath.

"I give no heed to the idle gossip of servants, Susy," he said slowly. "I have no belief that you have ever contemplated anything worse than an act of girlish folly, or the gratification of a passing caprice. Neither do I want to appeal to you or frighten you, but I must tell you now, that I know certain facts that might make such a simple act of folly monstrous, inconceivable in YOU, and almost accessory to a crime! I can tell you no more. But so satisfied am I of such a possibility, that I shall not scruple to take any means—the strongest—to prevent even the remotest chance of it. Your aunt has been looking for you; you had better go to her now. I will close the room and lock the door. Meantime, I should advise you not to sit so near an open window with a candle at night in this locality. Even if it might not be dangerous for you, it might be fatal to the foolish creatures it might attract."

He took the key from the door as he held it open for her to pass out. She uttered a shrill little laugh, like a nervous, mischievous child, and, slipping out of her previous artificial attitude as if it had been a mantle, ran out of the room.

CHAPTER X

As Susy's footsteps died away, Clarence closed the door, walked to the window, and examined it closely. The bars had been restored since he had wrenched them off to give ingress to the family on the day of recapture. He glanced around the room; nothing seemed to have been disturbed. Nevertheless he was uneasy. The suspicions of a frank, trustful nature when once aroused are apt to be more general and far-reaching than the specific distrusts of the disingenuous, for they imply the overthrow of a whole principle and not a mere detail. Clarence's conviction that Susy had seen Pedro recently since his dismissal led him into the wildest surmises of her motives. It was possible that without her having reason to suspect Pedro's greater crime, he might have confided to her his intention of reclaiming the property and installing her as the mistress and chatelaine of the rancho. The idea was one that might have appealed to Susy's theatrical imagination. He recalled Mrs. McClosky's sneer at his own pretensions and her vague threats of a rival of more lineal descent. The possible infidelity of Susy to himself touched him lightly when the first surprise was over; indeed, it scarcely could be called infidelity, if she knew and believed Mary Rogers's discovery; and the conviction that he and she had really never loved each other now enabled him, as he believed, to look at her conduct dispassionately. Yet it was her treachery to Mrs. Peyton and not to himself that impressed him most, and perhaps made him equally unjust, through his affections.

He extinguished the candles, partly from some vague precautions he could not explain, and partly to think over his fears in the abstraction and obscurity of the semi-darkness. The higher windows suffused a faint light on the ceiling, and, assisted by the dark lantern-like glow cast on the opposite wall by the tunnel of the embrasured window, the familiar outlines of the room and its furniture came back to him. Somewhat in this fashion also, in the obscurity and quiet, came back to him the events he had overlooked and forgotten. He recalled now some gossip of the servants, and hints dropped by Susy of a violent quarrel between Peyton and Pedro, which resulted in Pedro's dismissal, but which now seemed clearly attributable to some graver cause than inattention and insolence. He recalled Mary Rogers's playful pleasantries with Susy about Pedro, and Susy's mysterious air, which he had hitherto regarded only as part of her exaggeration. He remembered Mrs. Peyton's unwarrantable uneasiness about Susy, which he had either overlooked or referred entirely to himself; she must have suspected something. To his quickened imagination, in this ruin of his faith and trust, he believed that Hooker's defection was either part of the conspiracy, or that he had run away to avoid being implicated with Susy in its discovery. This, too, was the significance of Gilroy's parting warning. He and Mrs. Peyton alone had been blind and confiding in the midst of this treachery, and even HE had been blind to his own real affections.

The wind had risen again, and the faint light on the opposite wall grew tremulous and shifting with the movement of the foliage without. But presently the glow became quite obliterated, as if by the intervention of some opaque body outside the window. He rose hurriedly and went to the casement. But at the same moment he fancied he heard the jamming of a door or window in quite another direction, and his examination of the casement before him showed him only the silver light of the thinly clouded sky falling uninterruptedly through the bars and foliage on the interior of the whitewashed embrasure. Then a conception of his mistake flashed across him. The line of the casa was long, straggling, and exposed elsewhere; why should the attempt to enter or communicate with any one within be confined only to this single point? And why not satisfy himself at once if any trespassers were lounging around the walls, and then confront them boldly in the open? Their discovery and identification was as important as the defeat of their intentions.

He relit the candle, and, placing it on a small table by the wall beyond the visual range of the window, rearranged the curtain so that, while it permitted the light to pass out, it left the room in shadow. He then opened the door softly, locked it behind him, and passed noiselessly into the hall. Susy's and Mrs. McClosky's rooms were at the further end of the passage, but between them and the boudoir was the open patio, and the low murmur of the voices of servants, who still lingered until he should dismiss them for the night. Turning back, he moved silently down the passage, until he reached the narrow arched door to the garden. This he unlocked and opened with the same stealthy caution. The rain had recommenced. Not daring to risk a return to his room, he took from a peg in the recess an old waterproof cloak and "sou'wester" of Peyton's, which still hung there, and passed out into the night, locking the door behind him. To keep the knowledge of his secret patrol from the stablemen, he did not attempt to take out his own horse, but trusted to find some vacquero's mustang in the corral. By good luck an old "Blue Grass" hack of Peyton's, nearest the stockade as he entered, allowed itself to be quickly caught. Using its rope headstall for a bridle, Clarence vaulted on its bare back, and paced cautiously out into the road. Here he kept the curve of the long line of stockade until he reached the outlying field where, half hidden in the withered, sapless, but still standing stalks of grain, he slowly began a circuit of the casa.

The misty gray dome above him, which an invisible moon seemed to have quicksilvered over, alternately lightened and darkened with passing gusts of fine rain. Nevertheless he could see the outline of the broad quadrangle of the house quite distinctly, except on the west side, where a fringe of writhing willows beat the brown adobe walls with their imploring arms at every gust. Elsewhere nothing moved; the view was uninterrupted to where the shining, watery sky met the equally shining, watery plain. He had already made a half circuit of the house, and was still noiselessly picking his way along the furrows, muffled with soaked and broken-down blades, and the velvety upspringing of the "volunteer" growth, when suddenly, not fifty yards before him, without sound or warning, a figure rode out of the grain upon the open crossroad, and deliberately halted with a listless, abstracted, waiting air. Clarence instantly recognized one of his own vacqueros, an undersized half-breed, but he as instantly divined that he was only an outpost or confederate, stationed to give the alarm. The same precaution had prevented each hearing the other, and the lesser height of the vacquero had rendered him indistinguishable as he preceded Clarence among the grain. As the young man made no doubt that the real trespasser was nearer the casa, along the line of willows, he wheeled to intercept him without alarming his sentry. Unfortunately, his horse answered the rope bridle clumsily, and splashed in striking out. The watcher quickly raised his head, and Clarence knew that his only chance was now to suppress him. Determined to do this at any hazard, with a threatening gesture he charged boldly down upon him.

But he had not crossed half the distance between them when the man uttered an appalling cry, so wild and despairing that it seemed to chill even the hot blood in Clarence's veins, and dashed frenziedly down the cross-road into the interminable plain. Before Clarence could determine if that cry was a signal or an involuntary outburst, it was followed instantly by the sound of frightened and struggling hoofs clattering against the wall of the casa, and a swaying of the shrubbery near the back gate of the patio. Here was his real quarry! Without hesitation he dug his heels into the flanks of his horse and rode furiously towards it. As he approached, a long tremor seemed to pass through the shrubbery, with the retreating sound of horse hoofs. The unseen trespasser had evidently taken the alarm and was fleeing, and Clarence dashed in pursuit. Following the sound, for the shrubbery hid the fugitive from view, he passed the last wall of the casa; but it soon became evident that the unknown had the better horse. The hoof-beats grew fainter and fainter, and at times appeared even to cease, until his own approach started them again, eventually to fade away in the distance. In vain Clarence dug his heels into the flanks of his heavier steed, and regretted his own mustang; and when at last he reached the edge of the thicket he had lost both sight and sound of the fugitive. The descent to the lower terrace lay before him empty and desolate. The man had escaped!

He turned slowly back with baffled anger and vindictiveness. However, he had prevented something, although he knew not what. The principal had got away, but he had identified his confederate, and for the first time held a clue to his mysterious visitant. There was no use to alarm the household, which did not seem to have been disturbed. The trespassers were far away by this time, and the attempt would hardly be repeated that night. He made his way quietly back to the corral, let loose his horse, and regained the casa unobserved. He unlocked the arched door in the wall, reentered the darkened passage, stopped a moment to open the door of the boudoir, glance at the closely fastened casement, and extinguish the still burning candle, and, relocking the door securely, made his way to his own room.

But he could not sleep. The whole incident, over so quickly, had nevertheless impressed him deeply, and yet like a dream. The strange yell of the vacquero still rang in his ears, but with an unearthly and superstitious significance that was even more dreamlike in its meaning. He awakened from a fitful slumber to find the light of morning in the room, and Incarnacion standing by his bedside.

The yellow face of the steward was greenish with terror, and his lips were dry.

"Get up, Senor Clarencio; get up at once, my master. Strange things have happened. Mother of God protect us!"

Clarence rolled to his feet, with the events of the past night struggling back upon his consciousness.

"What mean you, Nascio?" he said, grasping the man's arm, which was still mechanically making the sign of the cross, as he muttered incoherently. "Speak, I command you!"

"It is Jose, the little vacquero, who is even now at the padre's house, raving as a lunatic, stricken as a madman with terror! He has seen him—the dead alive! Save us!"

"Are you mad yourself, Nascio?" said Clarence. "Whom has he seen?"

"Whom? God help us! the old padron—Senor Peyton himself! He rushed towards him here, in the patio, last night—out of the air, the sky, the ground, he knew not—his own self, wrapped in his old storm cloak and hat, and riding his own horse—erect, terrible, and menacing, with an awful hand upholding a rope—so! He saw him with these eyes, as I see you. What HE said to him, God knows! The priest, perhaps, for he has made confession!"

In a flash of intelligence Clarence comprehended all. He rose grimly and began to dress himself.

"Not a word of this to the women—to any one, Nascio, dost thou understand?" he said curtly. "It may be that Jose has been partaking too freely of aguardiente—it is possible. I will see the priest myself. But what possesses thee? Collect thyself, good Nascio."

But the man was still trembling.

"It is not all—Mother of God! it is not all, master!" he stammered, dropping to his knees and still crossing himself. "This morning, beside the corral, they find the horse of Pedro Valdez splashed and spattered on saddle and bridle, and in the stirrup—dost thou hear? the STIRRUP—hanging, the torn-off boot of Valdez! Ah, God! The same as HIS! Now do you understand? It is HIS vengeance. No! Jesu forgive me! it is the vengeance of God!"

Clarence was staggered.

"And you have not found Valdez? You have looked for him?" he said, hurriedly throwing on his clothes.

"Everywhere—all over the plain. The whole rancho has been out since sunrise—here and there and everywhere. And there is nothing! Of course not. What would you?" He pointed solemnly to the ground.

"Nonsense!" said Clarence, buttoning his coat and seizing his hat. "Follow me."

He ran down the passage, followed by Incarnacion, through the excited, gesticulating crowd of servants in the patio, and out of the back gate. He turned first along the wall of the casa towards the barred window of the boudoir. Then a cry came from Incarnacion.

They ran quickly forward. Hanging from the grating of the window, like a mass of limp and saturated clothes, was the body of Pedro Valdez, with one unbooted foot dangling within an inch of the ground. His head was passed inside the grating and fixed as at that moment when the first spring of the frightened horse had broken his neck between the bars as in a garrote, and the second plunge of the terrified animal had carried off his boot in the caught stirrup when it escaped.

CHAPTER XI

The winter rains were over and gone, and the whole long line of Californian coast was dashed with color. There were miles of yellow and red poppies, leagues of lupines that painted the gently rounded hills with soft primary hues, and long continuous slopes, like low mountain systems, of daisies and dandelions. At Sacramento it was already summer; the yellow river was flashing and intolerable; the tule and marsh grasses were lush and long; the bloom of cottonwood and sycamore whitened the outskirts of the city, and as Cyrus Hopkins and his daughter Phoebe looked from the veranda of the Placer Hotel, accustomed as they were to the cool trade winds of the coast valleys, they felt homesick from the memory of eastern heats.

Later, when they were surveying the long dinner tables at the table d'hote with something of the uncomfortable and shamefaced loneliness of the provincial, Phoebe uttered a slight cry and clutched her father's arm. Mr. Hopkins stayed the play of his squared elbows and glanced inquiringly at his daughter's face. There was a pretty animation in it, as she pointed to a figure that had just entered. It was that of a young man attired in the extravagance rather than the taste of the prevailing fashion, which did not, however, in the least conceal a decided rusticity of limb and movement. A long mustache, which looked unkempt, even in its pomatumed stiffness, and lank, dark hair that had bent but never curled under the barber's iron, made him notable even in that heterogeneous assembly.

"That's he," whispered Phoebe.

"Who?" said her father.

Alas for the inconsistencies of love! The blush came with the name and not the vision.

"Mr. Hooker," she stammered.

It was, indeed, Jim Hooker. But the role of his exaggeration was no longer the same; the remorseful gloom in which he had been habitually steeped had changed into a fatigued, yet haughty, fastidiousness more in keeping with his fashionable garments. He was more peaceful, yet not entirely placable, and, as he sat down at a side table and pulled down his striped cuffs with his clasped fingers, he cast a glance of critical disapproval on the general company. Nevertheless, he seemed to be furtively watchful of his effect upon them, and as one or two whispered and looked towards him, his consciousness became darkly manifest.

All of which might have intimidated the gentle Phoebe, but did not discompose her father. He rose, and crossing over to Hooker's table, clapped him heartily on the back.

"How do, Hooker? I didn't recognize you in them fine clothes, but Phoebe guessed as how it was you."

Flushed, disconcerted, irritated, but always in wholesome awe of Mr. Hopkins, Jim returned his greeting awkwardly and half hysterically. How he would have received the more timid Phoebe is another question. But Mr. Hopkins, without apparently noticing these symptoms, went on:—

"We're only just down, Phoebe and me, and as I guess we'll want to talk over old times, we'll come alongside o' you. Hold on, and I'll fetch her."

The interval gave the unhappy Jim a chance to recover himself, to regain his vanished cuffs, display his heavy watch-chain, curl his mustache, and otherwise reassume his air of blase fastidiousness. But the transfer made, Phoebe, after shaking hands, became speechless under these perfections. Not so her father.

"If there's anything in looks, you seem to be prospering," he said grimly; "unless you're in the tailorin' line, and you're only showin' off stock. What mout ye be doing?"

"Ye ain't bin long in Sacramento, I reckon?" suggested Jim, with patronizing pity.

"No, we only came this morning," returned Hopkins.

"And you ain't bin to the theatre?" continued Jim.

"No."

"Nor moved much in—in—gin'ral fash'nable sassiety?"

"Not yet," interposed Phoebe, with an air of faint apology.

"Nor seen any of them large posters on the fences, of 'The Prairie Flower; or, Red-handed Dick,'—three-act play with five tableaux—just the biggest sensation out—runnin' for forty nights—money turned away every night—standin' room only?" continued Jim, with prolonged toleration.

"No."

"Well, I play Red-handed Dick. I thought you might have seen it and recognized me. All those people over there," darkly indicating the long table, "know me. A fellow can't stand it, you know, being stared at by such a vulgar, low-bred lot. It's gettin' too fresh here. I'll have to give the landlord notice and cut the whole hotel. They don't seem to have ever seen a gentleman and a professional before."

"Then you're a play-actor now?" said the farmer, in a tone which did not, however, exhibit the exact degree of admiration which shone in Phoebe's eyes.

"For the present," said Jim, with lofty indifference. "You see I was in—in partnership with McClosky, the manager, and I didn't like the style of the chump that was doin' Red-handed Dick, so I offered to take his place one night to show him how. And by Jinks! the audience, after that night, wouldn't let anybody else play it—wouldn't stand even the biggest, highest-priced stars in it! I reckon," he added gloomily, "I'll have to run the darned thing in all the big towns in Californy—if I don't have to go East with it after all, just for the business. But it's an awful grind on a man—leaves him no time, along of the invitations he gets, and what with being run after in the streets and stared at in the hotels he don't get no privacy. There's men, and women, too, over at that table, that just lie in wait for me here till I come, and don't lift their eyes off me. I wonder they don't bring their opery-glasses with them."

Concerned, sympathizing, and indignant, poor Phoebe turned her brown head and honest eyes in that direction. But because they were honest, they could not help observing that the other table did not seem to be paying the slightest attention to the distinguished impersonator of Red-handed

Dick. Perhaps he had been overheard.

"Then that was the reason ye didn't come back to your location. I always guessed it was because you'd got wind of the smash-up down there, afore we did," said Hopkins grimly.

"What smash-up?" asked Jim, with slightly resentful quickness.

"Why, the smash-up of the Sisters' title—didn't you hear that?"

There was a slight movement of relief and a return of gloomy hauteur in Jim's manner.

"No, we don't know much of what goes on in the cow counties, up here."

"Ye mout, considerin' it concerns some o' your friends," returned Hopkins dryly. "For the Sisters' title went smash as soon as it was known that Pedro Valdez—the man as started it—had his neck broken outside the walls o' Robles Rancho; and they do say as this yer Brant, YOUR friend, had suthin' to do with the breaking of it, though it was laid to the ghost of old Peyton. Anyhow, there was such a big skeer that one of the Greaser gang, who thought he'd seen the ghost, being a Papist, to save his everlasting soul went to the priest and confessed. But the priest wouldn't give him absolution until he'd blown the hull thing, and made it public. And then it turned out that all the dockyments for the title, and even the custom-house paper, were FORGED by Pedro Valdez, and put on the market by his confederates. And that's just where YOUR friend, Clarence Brant, comes in, for HE had bought up the whole title from them fellers. Now, either, as some say, he was in the fraud from the beginnin', and never paid anything, or else he was an all-fired fool, and had parted with his money like one. Some allow that the reason was that he was awfully sweet on Mrs. Peyton's adopted daughter, and ez the parents didn't approve of him, he did THIS so as to get a holt over them by the property. But he's a ruined man, anyway, now; for they say he's such a darned fool that he's goin' to pay for all the improvements that the folks who bought under him put into the land, and that'll take his last cent. I thought I'd tell you that, for I suppose YOU'VE lost a heap in your improvements, and will put in your claim?"

"I reckon I put nearly as much into it as Clar Brant did," said Jim gloomily, "but I ain't goin' to take a cent from him, or go back on him now."

The rascal could not resist this last mendacious opportunity, although he was perfectly sincere in his renunciation, touched in his sympathy, and there was even a film of moisture in his shifting eyes.

Phoebe was thrilled with the generosity of this noble being, who could be unselfish even in his superior condition. She added softly:—

"And they say that the girl did not care for him at all, but was actually going to run off with Pedro, when he stopped her and sent for Mrs. Peyton."

To her surprise, Jim's face flushed violently.

"It's all a dod-blasted lie," he said, in a thick stage whisper. "It's only the hogwash them Greasers and Pike County galoots ladle out to each other around the stove in a county grocery. But," recalling himself loftily, and with a tolerant wave of his be-diamonded hand, "wot kin you expect from one of them cow counties? They ain't satisfied till they drive every gentleman out of the darned gopher-holes they call their 'kentry.'"

In her admiration of what she believed to be a loyal outburst for his friend, Phoebe overlooked the implied sneer at her provincial home. But her father went on with a perfunctory, exasperating, dusty aridity:—

"That mebbee ez mebbee, Mr. Hooker, but the story down in our precinct goes that she gave Mrs. Peyton the slip—chucked up her situation as adopted darter, and went off with a queer sort of a cirkiss woman—one of her own KIN, and I reckon one of her own KIND."

To this Mr. Hooker offered no further reply than a withering rebuke of the waiter, a genteel abstraction, and a lofty change of subject. He pressed upon them two tickets for the performance, of which he seemed to have a number neatly clasped in an india-rubber band, and advised them to come early. They would see him after the performance and sup together. He must leave them now, as he had to be punctually at the theatre, and if he lingered he should be pestered by interviewers. He withdrew under a dazzling display of cuff and white handkerchief, and with that inward swing of the arm and slight bowiness of the leg generally recognized in his profession as the lounging exit of high comedy.

The mingling of awe and an uneasy sense of changed relations which that meeting with Jim had brought to Phoebe was not lessened when she entered the theatre with her father that evening, and even Mr. Hopkins seemed to share her feelings. The theatre was large, and brilliant in decoration, the seats were well filled with the same heterogeneous mingling she had seen in the dining-room at the Placer Hotel, but in the parquet were some fashionable costumes and cultivated faces. Mr. Hopkins was not altogether so sure that Jim had been "only gassing." But the gorgeous drop curtain, representing an allegory of Californian prosperity and abundance, presently uprolled upon a scene of Western life almost as striking in its glaring unreality. From a rose-clad English cottage in a subtropical landscape skipped "Rosalie, the Prairie Flower." The briefest of skirts, the most unsullied of stockings, the tiniest of slippers, and the few diamonds that glittered on her fair neck and fingers, revealed at once the simple and unpretending daughter of the American backwoodsman. A tumult of delighted greeting broke from the audience. The bright color came to the pink, girlish cheeks, gratified vanity danced in her violet eyes, and as she piquantly bowed her acknowledgments, this great breath of praise seemed to transfigure and possess her. A very young actor who represented the giddy world in a straw hat and with an effeminate manner was alternately petted and girded at by her during the opening exposition of the plot, until the statement that a "dark destiny" obliged her to follow her uncle in an emigrant train across the plains closed the act, apparently extinguished him, and left HER the central figure. So far, she evidently was the favorite. A singular aversion to her crept into the heart of Phoebe.

But the second act brought an Indian attack upon the emigrant train, and here "Rosalie" displayed the archest heroism and the pinkest and most distracting self-possession, in marked contrast to the giddy worldling who, having accompanied her apparently for comic purposes best known to himself, cowered abjectly under wagons, and was pulled ignominiously out of straw, until Red Dick swept out of the wings with a chosen band and a burst of revolvers and turned the tide of victory. Attired as a picturesque combination of the Neapolitan smuggler, river-bar miner, and Mexican vacquero, Jim Hooker instantly began to justify the plaudits that greeted him and the most sanguinary hopes of the audience. A gloomy but fascinating cloud of gunpowder and dark intrigue from that moment hung about the stage.

Yet in this sombre obscuration Rosalie had passed a happy six months, coming out with her character and stockings equally unchanged and unblemished, to be rewarded with the hand of Red Dick and the discovery of her father, the governor of New Mexico, as a white-haired, but objectionable vacquero, at the fall of the curtain.

Through this exciting performance Phoebe sat with a vague and increasing sense of loneliness and distrust. She did not know that Hooker had added to his ordinary inventive exaggeration the form of dramatic composition. But she had early detected the singular fact that such shadowy outlines of plot as the piece possessed were evidently based on his previous narrative of his OWN experiences, and the saving of Susy Peyton—by himself! There was the episode of their being lost on the plains, as he had already related it to her, with the addition of a few years to Susy's age and some vivid picturesqueness to himself as Red Dick. She was not, of course, aware that the part of the giddy worldling was Jim's own conception of the character of Clarence. But what, even to her provincial taste, seemed the extravagance of the piece, she felt, in some way, reflected upon the truthfulness of the story she had heard. It seemed to be a parody on himself, and in the laughter which some of the most thrilling points produced in certain of the audience, she heard an echo of her own doubts. But even this she could have borne if Jim's confidence had not been given to the general public; it was no longer HERS alone, she shared it with them. And this strange, bold girl, who acted with him—the "Blanche Belville" of the bills—how often he must have told HER the story, and yet how badly she had learned it! It was not her own idea of it, nor of HIM. In the last extravagant scene she turned her weary and half-shamed eyes from the stage and looked around the theatre. Among a group of loungers by the wall a face that seemed familiar was turned towards her own with a look of kindly and sympathetic recognition. It was the face of Clarence Brant. When the curtain fell, and she and her father rose to go, he was at their side. He seemed older and more superior looking than she had ever thought him before, and there was a gentle yet sad wisdom in his eyes and voice that comforted her even while it made her feel like crying.

"You are satisfied that no harm has come to our friend," he said pleasantly. "Of course you recognized him?"

"Oh, yes; we met him to-day," said Phoebe. Her provincial pride impelled her to keep up a show of security and indifference. "We are going to supper with him."

Clarence slightly lifted his brows.

"You are more fortunate than I am," he said smilingly. "I only arrived here at seven, and I must leave at midnight."

Phoebe hesitated a moment, then said with affected carelessness:—

"What do you think of the young girl who plays with him? Do you know her? Who is she?"

He looked at her quickly, and then said, with some surprise:—

"Did he not tell you?"

"She WAS the adopted daughter of Mrs. Peyton—Miss Susan Silsbee," he said gravely.

"Then she DID run away from home as they said," said Phoebe impulsively.

"Not EXACTLY as they said," said Clarence gently. "She elected to make her home with her aunt, Mrs. McClosky, who is the wife of the manager of this theatre, and she adopted the profession a month ago. As it now appears that there was some informality in the old articles of guardianship, Mrs. Peyton would have been powerless to prevent her from doing either, even if she had wished to."

The infelicity of questioning Clarence regarding Susy suddenly flashed upon the forgetful Phoebe, and she colored. Yet, although sad, he did not look like a rejected lover.

"Of course, if she is here with her own relatives, that makes all the difference," she said gently. "It is protection."

"Certainly," said Clarence.

"And," continued Phoebe hesitatingly, "she is playing with— with—an old friend—Mr. Hooker!"

"That is quite proper, too, considering their relations," said Clarence tolerantly.

"I—don't—understand," stammered Phoebe.

The slightly cynical smile on Clarence's face changed as he looked into Phoebe's eyes.

"I've just heard that they are married," he returned gently.

CHAPTER XII

Nowhere had the long season of flowers brought such glory as to the broad plains and slopes of Robles Rancho. By some fortuitous chance of soil, or flood, or drifting pollen, the three terraces had each taken a distinct and separate blossom and tint of color. The straggling line of corral, the crumbling wall of the old garden, the outlying chapel, and even the brown walls of the casa itself, were half sunken in the tall racemes of crowding lupines, until from the distance they seemed to be slowly settling in the profundity of a dark-blue sea. The second terrace was a league-long flow of gray and gold daisies, in which the cattle dazedly wandered mid-leg deep. A perpetual sunshine of yellow dandelions lay upon the third. The gentle slope to the dark-green canada was a broad cataract of crimson poppies. Everywhere where water had stood, great patches of color had taken its place. It seemed as if the rains had ceased only that the broken heavens might drop flowers.

Never before had its beauty—a beauty that seemed built upon a cruel, youthful, obliterating forgetfulness of the past—struck Clarence as keenly as when he had made up his mind that he must leave the place forever. For the tale of his mischance and ill-fortune, as told by Hopkins, was unfortunately true. When he discovered that in his desire to save Peyton's house by the purchase of the Sisters' title he himself had been the victim of a gigantic fraud, he accepted the loss of the greater part of his fortune with resignation, and was even satisfied by the thought that he had at least effected the possession of the property for Mrs. Peyton. But when he found that those of his tenants who had bought under him had acquired only a dubious possession of their lands and no title, he had unhesitatingly reimbursed them for their improvements with the last of his capital. Only the lawless Gilroy had good-humoredly declined. The quiet acceptance of the others did not, unfortunately, preclude their settled belief that Clarence had participated in the fraud, and that even now his restitution was making a dangerous precedent, subversive of the best interests of the State, and discouraging to immigration. Some doubted his sanity. Only one, struck with the sincerity of his motive, hesitated to take his money, with a look of commiseration on his face.

"Are you not satisfied?" asked Clarence, smiling.

"Yes, but"—

"But what?"

"Nothin'. Only I was thinkin' that a man like you must feel awful lonesome in Calforny!"

Lonely he was, indeed; but his loneliness was not the loss of fortune nor what it might bring. Perhaps he had never fully realized his wealth; it had been an accident rather than a custom of his life, and when it had failed in the only test he had made of its power, it is to be feared that he only sentimentally regretted it. It was too early yet for him to comprehend the veiled blessings of the catastrophe in its merciful disruption of habits and ways of life; his loneliness was still the hopeless solitude left by vanished ideals and overthrown idols. He was satisfied that he had never cared for Susy, but he still cared for the belief that he had.

After the discovery of Pedro's body that fatal morning, a brief but emphatic interview between himself and Mrs. McClosky had followed. He had insisted upon her immediately accompanying Susy and himself to Mrs. Peyton in San Francisco. Horror-stricken and terrified at the catastrophe, and frightened by the strange looks of the excited servants, they did not dare to disobey him. He had left them with Mrs. Peyton in the briefest preliminary interview, during which he spoke only of the catastrophe, shielding the woman from the presumption of having provoked it, and urging only the importance of settling the question of guardianship at once. It was odd that Mrs. Peyton had been less disturbed than he imagined she would be at even his charitable version of Susy's unfaithfulness to her; it even seemed to him that she had already suspected it. But as he was about to withdraw to leave her to meet them alone, she had stopped him suddenly.

"What would you advise me to do?"

It was his first interview with her since the revelation of his own feelings. He looked into the pleading, troubled eyes of the woman he now knew he had loved, and stammered:—

"You alone can judge. Only you must remember that one cannot force an affection any more than one can prevent it."

He felt himself blushing, and, conscious of the construction of his words, he even fancied that she was displeased.

"Then you have no preference?" she said, a little impatiently.

"None."

She made a slight gesture with her handsome shoulders, but

she only said, "I should have liked to have pleased you in this," and turned coldly away. He had left without knowing the result of the interview; but a few days later he received a letter from her stating that she had allowed Susy to return to her aunt, and that she had resigned all claims to her guardianship.

"It seemed to be a foregone conclusion," she wrote; "and although I cannot think such a change will be for her permanent welfare, it is her present WISH, and who knows, indeed, if the change will be permanent? I have not allowed the legal question to interfere with my judgment, although her friends must know that she forfeits any claim upon the estate by her action; but at the same time, in the event of her suitable marriage, I should try to carry out what I believe would have been Mr. Peyton's wishes."

There were a few lines of postscript: "It seems to me that the change would leave you more free to consult your own wishes in regard to continuing your friendship with Susy, and upon such a footing as may please you. I judge from Mrs. McClosky's conversation that she believed you thought you were only doing your duty in reporting to me, and that the circumstances had not altered the good terms in which you all three formerly stood."

Clarence had dropped the letter with a burning indignation that seemed to sting his eyes until a scalding moisture hid the words before him. What might not Susy have said? What exaggeration of his affection was she not capable of suggesting? He recalled Mrs. McClosky, and remembered her easy acceptance of him as Susy's lover. What had they told Mrs. Peyton? What must be her opinion of his deceit towards herself? It was hard enough to bear this before he knew he loved her. It was intolerable now! And this is what she meant when she suggested that he should renew his old terms with Susy; it was for HIM that this ill-disguised, scornful generosity in regard to Susy's pecuniary expectations was intended. What should he do? He would write to her, and indignantly deny any clandestine affection for Susy. But could he do that, in honor, in truthfulness? Would it not be better to write and confess all? Yes—EVERYTHING.

Fortunately for his still boyish impulsiveness, it was at this time that the discovery of his own financial ruin came to him. The inquest on the body of Pedro Valdez and the confession of his confidant had revealed the facts of the fraudulent title and forged testamentary documents. Although it was correctly believed that Pedro had met his death in an escapade of gallantry or intrigue, the coroner's jury had returned a verdict of "accidental death," and the lesser scandal was lost in the wider, far-spreading disclosure of fraud. When he had resolved to assume all the liabilities of his purchase, he was obliged to write to Mrs. Peyton and confess his ruin. But he was glad to remind her that it did not alter HER status or security; he had only given her the possession, and she would revert to her original and now uncontested title. But as there was now no reason for his continuing the stewardship, and as he must adopt some profession and seek his fortune elsewhere, he begged her to relieve him of his duty. Albeit written with a throbbing heart and suffused eyes, it was a plain, business-like, and practical letter. Her reply was equally cool and matter of fact. She was sorry to hear of his losses, although she could not agree with him that they could logically sever his present connection with the rancho, or that, placed upon another and distinctly business footing, the occupation would not be as remunerative to him as any other. But, of course, if he had a preference for some more independent position, that was another question, although he would forgive her for using the privilege of her years to remind him that his financial and business success had not yet justified his independence. She

Bret Harte

would also advise him not to decide hastily, or, at least, to wait until she had again thoroughly gone over her husband's papers with her lawyer, in reference to the old purchase of the Sisters' title, and the conditions under which it was bought. She knew that Mr. Brant would not refuse this as a matter of business, nor would that friendship, which she valued so highly, allow him to imperil the possession of the rancho by leaving it at such a moment. As soon as she had finished the examination of the papers, she would write again. Her letter seemed to leave him no hope, if, indeed, he had ever indulged in any. It was the practical kindliness of a woman of business, nothing more. As to the examination of her husband's papers, that was a natural precaution. He alone knew that they would give no record of a transaction which had never occurred. He briefly replied that his intention to seek another situation was unchanged, but that he would cheerfully await the arrival of his successor. Two weeks passed. Then Mr. Sanderson, Mrs. Peyton's lawyer, arrived, bringing an apologetic note from Mrs. Peyton. She was so sorry her business was still delayed, but as she had felt that she had no right to detain him entirely at Robles, she had sent to Mr. Sanderson to TEMPORARILY relieve him, that he might be free to look around him or visit San Francisco in reference to his own business, only extracting a promise from him that he would return to Robles to meet her at the end of the week, before settling upon anything.

The bitter smile with which Clarence had read thus far suddenly changed. Some mysterious touch of unbusiness-like but womanly hesitation, that he had never noticed in her previous letters, gave him a faint sense of pleasure, as if her note had been perfumed. He had availed himself of the offer. It was on this visit to Sacramento that he had accidentally discovered the marriage of Susy and Hooker.

"It's a great deal better business for her to have a husband in the 'profesh' if she's agoin' to stick to it," said his informant, Mrs. McClosky, "and she's nothing if she ain't business and profesh, Mr. Brant. I never see a girl that was born for the stage—yes, you might say jess cut out o' the boards of the stage—as that girl Susy is! And that's jest what's the matter; and YOU know it, and I know it, and there you are!"

It was with these experiences that Clarence was to-day reentering the wooded and rocky gateway of the rancho from the high road of the canada; but as he cantered up the first slope, through the drift of scarlet poppies that almost obliterated the track, and the blue and yellow blooms of the terraces again broke upon his view, he thought only of Mrs. Peyton's pleasure in this changed aspect of her old home. She had told him of it once before, and of her delight in it; and he had once thought how happy he should be to see it with her.

The servant who took his horse told him that the senora had arrived that morning from Santa Inez, bringing with her the two Senoritas Hernandez from the rancho of Los Canejos, and that other guests were expected. And there was the Senor Sanderson and his Reverence Padre Esteban. Truly an affair of hospitality, the first since the padron died. Whatever dream Clarence might have had of opportunities for confidential interview was rudely dispelled. Yet Mrs. Peyton had left orders to be informed at once of Don Clarencio's arrival.

As he crossed the patio and stepped upon the corridor he fancied he already detected in the internal arrangements the subtle influence of Mrs. Peyton's taste and the indefinable domination of the mistress. For an instant he thought of anticipating the servant and seeking her in the boudoir, but some instinct withheld him, and he turned into the study which he had used as an office. It was empty; a few embers glimmered on the hearth. At the same moment there was a light step behind him, and Mrs. Peyton entered and closed the door behind her. She was very beautiful. Although paler and thinner, there was an odd sort of animation about her, so unlike her usual repose that it seemed almost feverish.

"I thought we could talk together a few moments before the guests arrive. The house will be presently so full, and my duties as hostess commence."

"I was—about to seek you—in—in the boudoir," hesitated Clarence.

She gave an impatient shiver.

"Good heavens, not there! I shall never go there again. I should fancy every time I looked out of the window that I saw the head of that man between the bars. No! I am only thankful that I wasn't here at the time, and that I can keep my remembrance of the dear old place unchanged." She checked herself a little abruptly, and then added somewhat irrelevantly but cheerfully, "Well, you have been away? What have you done?"

"Nothing," said Clarence.

"Then you have kept your promise," she said, with the same nervous hilarity.

"I have returned here without making any other engagement," he said gravely; "but I have not altered my determination."

She shrugged her shoulders again, or, as it seemed, the skin of her tightly fitting black dress above them, with the sensitive shiver of a highly groomed horse, and moved to the hearth as if for warmth; put her slim, slippered foot upon the low fender, drawing, with a quick hand, the whole width of her skirt behind her until it clingingly accented the long, graceful curve from her hip to her feet. All this was so unlike her usual fastidiousness and repose that he was struck by it. With her eyes on the glowing embers of the hearth, and tentatively advancing her toe to its warmth and drawing it away, she said:—

"Of course, you must please yourself. I am afraid I have no right except that of habit and custom to keep you here; and you know," she added, with an only half-withheld bitterness, "that they are not always very effective with young people who prefer to have the ordering of their own lives. But I have something still to tell you before you finally decide. I have, as you know, been looking over my—over Mr. Peyton's papers very carefully. Well, as a result, I find, Mr. Brant, that there is no record whatever of his wonderfully providential purchase of the Sisters' title from you; that he never entered into any written agreement with you, and never paid you a cent; and that, furthermore, his papers show me that he never even contemplated it; nor, indeed, even knew of YOUR owning the title when he died. Yes, Mr. Brant, it was all to YOUR foresight and prudence, and YOUR generosity alone, that we owe our present possession of the rancho. When you helped us into that awful window, it was YOUR house we were entering; and if it had been YOU, and not those wretches, who had chosen to shut the doors on us after the funeral, we could never have entered here again. Don't deny it, Mr. Brant. I have suspected it a long time, and when you spoke of changing YOUR position, I determined to find out if it wasn't I who had to leave the house rather than you. One moment, please. And I did find out, and it WAS I. Don't speak, please, yet. And now," she said, with a quick return to her previous nervous hilarity, "knowing this, as you did, and knowing, too, that I would know it when I examined the papers—don't speak, I'm not through yet—don't you think

Bret Harte

that it was just a LITTLE cruel for you to try to hurry me, and make me come here instead of your coming to ME in San Francisco, when I gave you leave for that purpose?"

"But, Mrs. Peyton," gasped Clarence.

"Please don't interrupt me," said the lady, with a touch of her old imperiousness, "for in a moment I must join my guests. When I found you wouldn't tell me, and left it to me to find out, I could only go away as I did, and really leave you to control what I believed was your own property. And I thought, too, that I understood your motives, and, to be frank with you, that worried me; for I believed I knew the disposition and feelings of a certain person better than yourself."

"One moment," broke out Clarence, "you MUST hear me, now. Foolish and misguided as that purchase may have been, I swear to you I had only one motive in making it—to save the homestead for you and your husband, who had been my first and earliest benefactors. What the result of it was, you, as a business woman, know; your friends know; your lawyer will tell you the same. You owe me nothing. I have given you nothing but the repossession of this property, which any other man could have done, and perhaps less stupidly than I did. I would not have forced you to come here to hear this if I had dreamed of your suspicions, or even if I had simply understood that you would see me in San Francisco as I passed through."

"Passed through? Where were you going?" she said quickly.

"To Sacramento."

The abrupt change in her manner startled him to a recollection of Susy, and he blushed. She bit her lips, and moved towards the window.

"Then you saw her?" she said, turning suddenly towards him. The inquiry of her beautiful eyes was more imperative than her speech.

Clarence recognized quickly what he thought was his cruel blunder in touching the half-healed wound of separation. But he had gone too far to be other than perfectly truthful now.

"Yes; I saw her on the stage," he said, with a return of his boyish earnestness; "and I learned something which I wanted you to first hear from me. She is MARRIED—and to Mr. Hooker, who is in the same theatrical company with her. But I want you to think, as I honestly do, that it is the best for her. She has married in her profession, which is a great protection and a help to her success, and she has married a man who can look lightly upon certain qualities in her that others might not be so lenient to. His worst faults are on the surface, and will wear away in contact with the world, and he looks up to her as his superior. I gathered this from her friend, for I did not speak with her myself; I did not go there to see her. But as I expected to be leaving you soon, I thought it only right that as I was the humble means of first bringing her into your life, I should bring you this last news, which I suppose takes her out of it forever. Only I want you to believe that YOU have nothing to regret, and that SHE is neither lost nor unhappy."

The expression of suspicious inquiry on her face when he began changed gradually to perplexity as he continued, and then relaxed into a faint, peculiar smile. But there was not the slightest trace of that pain, wounded pride, indignation, or anger, that he had expected to see upon it.

"That means, I suppose, Mr. Brant, that YOU no longer care

for her?"

The smile had passed, yet she spoke now with a half-real, half-affected archness that was also unlike her.

"It means," said Clarence with a white face, but a steady voice, "that I care for her now as much as I ever cared for her, no matter to what folly it once might have led me. But it means, also, that there was no time when I was not able to tell it to YOU as frankly as I do now"—

"One moment, please," she interrupted, and turned quickly towards the door. She opened it and looked out. "I thought they were calling me—and—I—I—MUST go now, Mr. Brant. And without finishing my business either, or saying half I had intended to say. But wait"—she put her hand to her head in a pretty perplexity, "it's a moonlight night, and I'll propose after dinner a stroll in the gardens, and you can manage to walk a little with me." She stopped again, returned, said, "It was very kind of you to think of me at Sacramento," held out her hand, allowed it to remain for an instant, cool but acquiescent, in his warmer grasp, and with the same odd youthfulness of movement and gesture slipped out of the door.

An hour later she was at the head of her dinner table, serene, beautiful, and calm, in her elegant mourning, provokingly inaccessible in the sweet deliberation of her widowed years; Padre Esteban was at her side with a local magnate, who had known Peyton and his wife, while Donna Rosita and a pair of liquid-tongued, childlike senoritas were near Clarence and Sanderson. To the priest Mrs. Peyton spoke admiringly of the changes in the rancho and the restoration of the Mission Chapel, and together they had commended Clarence from the level of their superior passionless reserve and years. Clarence felt hopelessly young and hopelessly lonely; the naive prattle of the young girls beside him appeared infantine. In his abstraction, he heard Mrs. Peyton allude to the beauty of the night, and propose that after coffee and chocolate the ladies should put on their wraps and go with her to the old garden. Clarence raised his eyes; she was not looking at him, but there was a slight consciousness in her face that was not there before, and the faintest color in her cheek, still lingering, no doubt, from the excitement of conversation.

It was a cool, tranquil, dewless night when they at last straggled out, mere black and white patches in the colorless moonlight. The brilliancy of the flower-hued landscape was subdued under its passive, pale austerity; even the gray and gold of the second terrace seemed dulled and confused. At any other time Clarence might have lingered over this strange effect, but his eyes followed only a tall figure, in a long striped burnous, that moved gracefully beside the soutaned priest. As he approached, it turned towards him.

"Ah! here you are. I just told Father Esteban that you talked of leaving to-morrow, and that he would have to excuse me a few moments while you showed me what you had done to the old garden."

She moved beside him, and, with a hesitation that was not unlike a more youthful timidity, slipped her hand through his arm. It was for the first time, and, without thinking, he pressed it impulsively to his side. I have already intimated that Clarence's reserve was at times qualified by singular directness.

A few steps carried them out of hearing; a few more, and they seemed alone in the world. The long adobe wall glanced away emptily beside them, and was lost; the black shadows of the knotted pear-trees were beneath their feet. They began to walk with the slight affectation of treading the shadows as if they were patterns on a carpet. Clarence was voiceless, and yet he seemed to be moving beside a spirit that must be first addressed.

But it was flesh and blood nevertheless.

"I interrupted you in something you were saying when I left the office," she said quietly.

"I was speaking of Susy," returned Clarence eagerly; "and"—

"Then you needn't go on," interrupted Mrs. Peyton quickly. "I understand you, and believe you. I would rather talk of something else. We have not yet arranged how I can make restitution to you for the capital you sank in saving this place. You will be reasonable, Mr. Brant, and not leave me with the shame and pain of knowing that you ruined yourself for the sake of your old friends. For it is no more a sentimental idea of mine to feel in this way than it is a fair and sensible one for you to imply that a mere quibble of construction absolves me from responsibility. Mr. Sanderson himself admits that the repossession you gave us is a fair and legal basis for any arrangement of sharing or division of the property with you, that might enable you to remain here and continue the work you have so well begun. Have you no suggestion, or must it come from ME, Mr. Brant?"

"Neither. Let us not talk of that now."

She did not seem to notice the boyish doggedness of his speech, except so far as it might have increased her inconsequent and nervously pitched levity.

"Then suppose we speak of the Misses Hernandez, with

whom you scarcely exchanged a word at dinner, and whom I invited for you and your fluent Spanish. They are charming girls, even if they are a little stupid. But what can I do? If I am to live here, I must have a few young people around me, if only to make the place cheerful for others. Do you know I have taken a great fancy to Miss Rogers, and have asked her to visit me. I think she is a good friend of yours, although perhaps she is a little shy. What's the matter? You have nothing against her, have you?"

Clarence had stopped short. They had reached the end of the pear-tree shadows. A few steps more would bring them to the fallen south wall of the garden and the open moonlight beyond, but to the right an olive alley of deeper shadow diverged.

"No," he said, with slow deliberation; "I have to thank Mary Rogers for having discovered something in me that I have been blindly, foolishly, and hopelessly struggling with."

"And, pray, what was that?" said Mrs. Peyton sharply.

"That I love you!"

Mrs. Peyton was fairly startled. The embarrassment of any truth is apt to be in its eternal abruptness, which no deviousness of tact or circumlocution of diplomacy has ever yet surmounted. Whatever had been in her heart, or mind, she was unprepared for this directness. The bolt had dropped from the sky; they were alone; there was nothing between the stars and the earth but herself and this man and this truth; it could not be overlooked, surmounted, or escaped from. A step or two more would take her out of the garden into the moonlight, but always into this awful frankness of blunt and outspoken nature. She hesitated, and turned the corner into the olive shadows. It was, perhaps, more dangerous; but less shameless, and less like truckling. And the appallingly direct Clarence instantly followed.

"I know you will despise me, hate me; and, perhaps, worst of all, disbelieve me; but I swear to you, now, that I have always loved you—yes, ALWAYS! When first I came here, it was not to see my old playmate, but YOU, for I had kept the memory of you as I first saw you when a boy, and you have always been my ideal. I have thought of, dreamed of, worshiped, and lived for no other woman. Even when I found Susy again, grown up here at your side; even when I thought that I might, with your consent, marry her, it was that I might be with YOU always; that I might be a part of YOUR home, your family, and have a place with her in YOUR heart; for it was you I loved, and YOU only. Don't laugh at me, Mrs. Peyton, it is the truth, the whole truth, I am telling you. God help me!"

If she only COULD have laughed—harshly, ironically, or even mercifully and kindly! But it would not come. And she burst out:—

"I am not laughing. Good heavens, don't you see? It is ME you are making ridiculous."

"YOU ridiculous?" he said in a momentarily choked, half-stupefied voice. "You—a beautiful woman, my superior in everything, the mistress of these lands where I am only steward—made ridiculous, not by my presumption, but by my confession? Was the saint you just now admired in Father Esteban's chapel ridiculous because of the peon clowns who were kneeling before it?"

"Hush! This is wicked! Stop!"

She felt she was now on firm ground, and made the most of

it in voice and manner. She must draw the line somewhere, and she would draw it between passion and impiety.

"Not until I have told you all, and I MUST before I leave you. I loved you when I came here—even when your husband was alive. Don't be angry, Mrs. Peyton; HE would not, and need not, have been angry; he would have pitied the foolish boy, who, in the very innocence and ignorance of his passion, might have revealed it to him as he did to everybody but ONE. And yet, I sometimes think you might have guessed it, had you thought of me at all. It must have been on my lips that day I sat with you in the boudoir. I know that I was filled with it; with it and with you; with your presence, with your beauty, your grace of heart and mind—yes, Mrs. Peyton, even with your own unrequited love for Susy. Only, then, I knew not what it was."

"But I think I can tell you what it was then, and now," said Mrs. Peyton, recovering her nervous little laugh, though it died a moment after on her lips. "I remember it very well. You told me then that I REMINDED YOU OF YOUR MOTHER. Well, I am not old enough to be your mother, Mr. Brant, but I am old enough to have been, and might have been, the mother of your wife. That was what you meant then; that is what you mean now. I was wrong to accuse you of trying to make me ridiculous. I ask your pardon. Let us leave it as it was that day in the boudoir, as it is NOW. Let me still remind you of your mother—I know she must have been a good woman to have had so good a son—and when you have found some sweet young girl to make you happy, come to me for a mother's blessing, and we will laugh at the recollection and misunderstanding of this evening."

Her voice did not, however, exhibit that exquisite maternal tenderness which the beatific vision ought to have called up, and the persistent voice of Clarence could not be evaded in the shadow.

"I said you reminded me of my mother," he went on at her side, "because I knew her and lost her only as a child. She never was anything to me but a memory, and yet an ideal of all that was sweet and lovable in woman. Perhaps it was a dream of what she might have been when she was as young in years as you. If it pleases you still to misunderstand me, it may please you also to know that there is a reminder of her even in this. I have no remembrance of a word of affection from her, nor a caress; I have been as hopeless in my love for her who was my mother, as of the woman I would make my wife."

"But you have seen no one, you know no one, you are young, you scarcely know your own self! You will forget this, you will forget ME! And if—if—I should—listen to you, what would the world say, what would YOU yourself say a few years hence? Oh, be reasonable. Think of it—it would be so wild—so mad! so—so—utterly ridiculous!"

In proof of its ludicrous quality, two tears escaped her eyes in the darkness. But Clarence caught the white flash of her withdrawn handkerchief in the shadow, and captured her returning hand. It was trembling, but did not struggle, and presently hushed itself to rest in his.

"I'm not only a fool but a brute," he said in a lower voice. "Forgive me. I have given you pain—you, for whom I would have died."

They had both stopped. He was still holding her sleeping hand. His arm had stolen around the burnous so softly that it followed the curves of her figure as lightly as a fold of the garment, and was presumably unfelt. Grief has its privileges, and suffering exonerates a questionable situation. In another moment her fair head MIGHT have dropped upon his shoulder. But an approaching voice uprose in the adjoining broad allee. It might have been the world speaking through the voice of the lawyer Sanderson.

"Yes, he is a good fellow, and an intelligent fellow, too, but a perfect child in his experience of mankind."

They both started, but Mrs. Peyton's hand suddenly woke up and grasped his firmly. Then she said in a higher, but perfectly level tone:—

"Yes, I think with you we had better look at it again in the sunlight to-morrow. But here come our friends; they have probably been waiting for us to join them and go in."

$$* \ * \ * \ * \ *$$

The wholesome freshness of early morning was in the room when Clarence awoke, cleared and strengthened. His resolution had been made. He would leave the rancho that morning, to enter the world again and seek his fortune elsewhere. This was only right to HER, whose future it should never be said he had imperiled by his folly and inexperience; and if, in a year or two of struggle he could prove his right to address her again, he would return. He had not spoken to her since they had parted in the garden, with the grim truths of the lawyer ringing in his ears, but he had written a few lines of farewell, to be given to her after he had left. He was calm in his resolution, albeit a little pale and hollow-eyed for it.

He crept downstairs in the gray twilight of the scarce-awakened house, and made his way to the stables. Saddling his horse, and mounting, he paced forth into the crisp morning air. The sun, just risen, was everywhere bringing out the fresh color of the flower-strewn terraces, as the last night's shadows, which had hidden them, were slowly beaten back. He cast a last look at the brown adobe quadrangle of the quiet house, just touched with the bronzing of the sun, and then turned his face towards the highway. As he passed the angle of the old garden he hesitated, but, strong in his resolution, he put the recollection of last night behind him, and rode by without raising his eyes.

"Clarence!"

It was HER voice. He wheeled his horse. She was standing behind the grille in the old wall as he had seen her standing on the day he had ridden to his rendezvous with Susy. A Spanish manta was thrown over her head and shoulders, as if she had dressed hastily, and had run out to intercept him while he was still in the stable. Her beautiful face was pale in its black-hooded recess, and there were faint circles around her lovely eyes.

"You were going without saying 'goodby'!" she said softly.

She passed her slim white hand between the grating. Clarence leaped to the ground, caught it, and pressed it to his lips. But he did not let it go.

"No! no!" she said, struggling to withdraw it. "It is better as it is—as—as you have decided it to be. Only I could not let you go thus—without a word. There now—go, Clarence, go. Please! Don't you see I am behind these bars? Think of them as the years that separate us, my poor, dear, foolish boy. Think of them as standing between us, growing closer, heavier, and more cruel and hopeless as the years go on."

Ah, well! they had been good bars a hundred and fifty years ago, when it was thought as necessary to repress the innocence that was behind them as the wickedness that was without. They had done duty in the convent at Santa Inez, and the monastery of Santa Barbara, and had been brought hither in Governor Micheltorrenas' time to keep the daughters of Robles from the insidious contact of the outer world, when they took the air in their cloistered pleasance. Guitars had tinkled against them in vain, and they had withstood the stress and storm of love tokens. But, like many other things which have had their day and time, they had retained their semblance of power, even while rattling loosely in their sockets, only because no one had ever thought of putting them to the test, and, in the strong hand of Clarence, assisted, perhaps, by the leaning figure of Mrs. Peyton, I grieve to say that the whole grille suddenly collapsed, became a frame of tinkling iron, and then clanked, bar by bar, into the road. Mrs. Peyton uttered a little cry and drew back, and Clarence, leaping the ruins, caught her in his arms.

For a moment only, for she quickly withdrew from them, and although the morning sunlight was quite rosy on her cheeks, she said gravely, pointing to the dismantled opening:—

"I suppose you MUST stay now, for you never could leave me here alone and defenseless."

He stayed. And with this fulfillment of his youthful dreams the romance of his young manhood seemed to be completed, and so closed the second volume of this trilogy. But what effect that fulfillment of youth had upon his maturer years, or the fortunes of those who were nearly concerned in it, may be told in a later and final chronicle.

ABOUT THE AUTHOR

Francis Bret Harte (August 25, 1836–May 6, 1902) was an American author and poet, best remembered for his accounts of pioneering life in California.

Born in Albany, New York, Harte moved to California in 1853, later working there in a number of capacities, including miner, teacher, messenger, and journalist. He spent part of his life in the northern California coast town now known as Arcata, at the time it was just a mining camp on Humboldt Bay.

His first literary efforts, including poetry and prose, appeared in The Californian, an early literary journal edited by Charles Henry Webb. In 1868 he became editor of The Overland Monthly, another new literary magazine, but this one more in tune with the pioneering spirit of excitement in California. His story, "The Luck of Roaring Camp," appeared in the magazine's second edition, propelling Harte to nationwide fame.

As an established literary figure, he was appointed to the position of United States Consul in the town of Krefeld, Germany in 1878 and Glasgow in 1880. In 1885 he settled in London. During the thirty years he spent in Europe, he never abandoned writing, and maintained a prodigious output of stories that retained the freshness of his earlier work. He died in England in 1902.

Other books by this author

Openings in the Old Trail
Sally Dows and Other Stories
Stories in Light and Shadow
Tales of the Argonauts
Tales of Trail and Town
The Three Partners
Under the Redwoods
By Shore and Sedge
Colonel Starbottle's Client and Other Stories
Clarence
Cressy
Devil's Ford
Frontier Stories
In a Hollow of the Hills
In the Carquinez Woods
Jeff Briggs's Love Story
Snow-Bound at Eagle's
The Argonauts of North Liberty
The Bell-Ringer of Angel's and Other Stories
The Crusade of the Excelsior
The Story of a Mine
Maruja

Choose from Thousands of 1stWorldLibrary Classics By

A. M. Barnard
Ada Leverson
Adolphus William Ward
Aesop
Agatha Christie
Alexander Aaronsohn
Alexander Kielland
Alexandre Dumas
Alfred Gatty
Alfred Ollivant
Alice Duer Miller
Alice Turner Curtis
Alice Dunbar
Allen Chapman
Alleyne Ireland
Ambrose Bierce
Amelia E. Barr
Amory H. Bradford
Andrew Lang
Andrew McFarland Davis
Andy Adams
Angela Brazil
Anna Alice Chapin
Anna Sewell
Annie Besant
Annie Hamilton Donnell
Annie Payson Call
Annie Roe Carr
Annonaymous
Anton Chekhov
Archibald Lee Fletcher
Arnold Bennett
Arthur C. Benson
Arthur Conan Doyle
Arthur M. Winfield
Arthur Ransome
Arthur Schnitzler
Arthur Train
Atticus
B.H. Baden-Powell
B. M. Bower
B. C. Chatterjee
Baroness Emmuska Orczy
Baroness Orczy
Basil King
Bayard Taylor
Ben Macomber
Bertha Muzzy Bower
Bjornstjerne Bjornson

Booth Tarkington
Boyd Cable
Bram Stoker
C. Collodi
C. E. Orr
C. M. Ingleby
Carolyn Wells
Catherine Parr Traill
Charles A. Eastman
Charles Amory Beach
Charles Dickens
Charles Dudley Warner
Charles Farrar Browne
Charles Ives
Charles Kingsley
Charles Klein
Charles Hanson Towne
Charles Lathrop Pack
Charles Romyn Dake
Charles Whibley
Charles Willing Beale
Charlotte M. Braeme
Charlotte M. Yonge
Charlotte Perkins Stetson
Clair W. Hayes
Clarence Day Jr.
Clarence E. Mulford
Clemence Housman
Confucius
Coningsby Dawson
Cornelis DeWitt Wilcox
Cyril Burleigh
D. H. Lawrence
Daniel Defoe
David Garnett
Dinah Craik
Don Carlos Janes
Donald Keyhoe
Dorothy Kilner
Dougan Clark
Douglas Fairbanks
E. Nesbit
E. P. Roe
E. Phillips Oppenheim
E. S. Brooks
Earl Barnes
Edgar Rice Burroughs
Edith Van Dyne
Edith Wharton

Edward Everett Hale
Edward J. O'Biren
Edward S. Ellis
Edwin L. Arnold
Eleanor Atkins
Eleanor Hallowell Abbott
Eliot Gregory
Elizabeth Gaskell
Elizabeth McCracken
Elizabeth Von Arnim
Ellem Key
Emerson Hough
Emilie F. Carlen
Emily Bronte
Emily Dickinson
Enid Bagnold
Enilor Macartney Lane
Erasmus W. Jones
Ernie Howard Pie
Ethel May Dell
Ethel Turner
Ethel Watts Mumford
Eugene Sue
Eugenie Foa
Eugene Wood
Eustace Hale Ball
Evelyn Everett-green
Everard Cotes
F. H. Cheley
F. J. Cross
F. Marion Crawford
Fannie E. Newberry
Federick Austin Ogg
Ferdinand Ossendowski
Fergus Hume
Florence A. Kilpatrick
Fremont B. Deering
Francis Bacon
Francis Darwin
Frances Hodgson Burnett
Frances Parkinson Keyes
Frank Gee Patchin
Frank Harris
Frank Jewett Mather
Frank L. Packard
Frank V. Webster
Frederic Stewart Isham
Frederick Trevor Hill
Frederick Winslow Taylor

Friedrich Kerst	Hayden Carruth	James Branch Cabell
Friedrich Nietzsche	Helent Hunt Jackson	James DeMille
Fyodor Dostoyevsky	Helen Nicolay	James Joyce
G.A. Henty	Hendrik Conscience	James Lane Allen
G.K. Chesterton	Hendy David Thoreau	James Lane Allen
Gabrielle E. Jackson	Henri Barbusse	James Oliver Curwood
Garrett P. Serviss	Henrik Ibsen	James Oppenheim
Gaston Leroux	Henry Adams	James Otis
George A. Warren	Henry Ford	James R. Driscoll
George Ade	Henry Frost	Jane Abbott
Geroge Bernard Shaw	Henry James	Jane Austen
George Cary Eggleston	Henry Jones Ford	Jane L. Stewart
George Durston	Henry Seton Merriman	Janet Aldridge
George Ebers	Henry W Longfellow	Jens Peter Jacobsen
George Eliot	Herbert A. Giles	Jerome K. Jerome
George Gissing	Herbert Carter	Jessie Graham Flower
George MacDonald	Herbert N. Casson	John Buchan
George Meredith	Herman Hesse	John Burroughs
George Orwell	Hildegard G. Frey	John Cournos
George Sylvester Viereck	Homer	John F. Kennedy
George Tucker	Honore De Balzac	John Gay
George W. Cable	Horace B. Day	John Glasworthy
George Wharton James	Horace Walpole	John Habberton
Gertrude Atherton	Horatio Alger Jr.	John Joy Bell
Gordon Casserly	Howard Pyle	John Kendrick Bangs
Grace E. King	Howard R. Garis	John Milton
Grace Gallatin	Hugh Lofting	John Philip Sousa
Grace Greenwood	Hugh Walpole	John Taintor Foote
Grant Allen	Humphry Ward	Jonas Lauritz Idemil Lie
Guillermo A. Sherwell	Ian Maclaren	Jonathan Swift
Gulielma Zollinger	Inez Haynes Gillmore	Joseph A. Altsheler
Gustav Flaubert	Irving Bacheller	Joseph Carey
H. A. Cody	Isabel Cecilia Williams	Joseph Conrad
H. B. Irving	Isabel Hornibrook	Joseph E. Badger Jr
H. C. Bailey	Israel Abrahams	Joseph Hergesheimer
H. G. Wells	Ivan Turgenev	Joseph Jacobs
H. H. Munro	J. G.Austin	Jules Vernes
H. Irving Hancock	J. Henri Fabre	Julian Hawthrone
H. R. Naylor	J. M. Barrie	Julie A Lippmann
H. Rider Haggard	J. M. Walsh	Justin Huntly McCarthy
H. W. C. Davis	J. Macdonald Oxley	Kakuzo Okakura
Haldeman Julius	J. R. Miller	Karle Wilson Baker
Hall Caine	J. S. Fletcher	Kate Chopin
Hamilton Wright Mabie	J. S. Knowles	Kenneth Grahame
Hans Christian Andersen	J. Storer Clouston	Kenneth McGaffey
Harold Avery	J. W. Duffield	Kate Langley Bosher
Harold McGrath	Jack London	Kate Langley Bosher
Harriet Beecher Stowe	Jacob Abbott	Katherine Cecil Thurston
Harry Castlemon	James Allen	Katherine Stokes
Harry Coghill	James Andrews	L. A. Abbot
Harry Houidini	James Baldwin	L. T. Meade

L. Frank Baum	Paul G. Tomlinson	T. S. Arthur
Latta Griswold	Paul Severing	The Princess Der Ling
Laura Dent Crane	Percy Brebner	Thomas A. Janvier
Laura Lee Hope	Percy Keese Fitzhugh	Thomas A Kempis
Laurence Housman	Peter B. Kyne	Thomas Anderton
Lawrence Beasley	Plato	Thomas Bailey Aldrich
Leo Tolstoy	Quincy Allen	Thomas Bulfinch
Leonid Andreyev	R. Derby Holmes	Thomas De Quincey
Lewis Carroll	R. L. Stevenson	Thomas Dixon
Lewis Sperry Chafer	R. S. Ball	Thomas H. Huxley
Lilian Bell	Rabindranath Tagore	Thomas Hardy
Lloyd Osbourne	Rahul Alvares	Thomas More
Louis Hughes	Ralph Bonehill	Thornton W. Burgess
Louis Joseph Vance	Ralph Henry Barbour	U. S. Grant
Louis Tracy	Ralph Victor	Upton Sinclair
Louisa May Alcott	Ralph Waldo Emmerson	Valentine Williams
Lucy Fitch Perkins	Rene Descartes	Various Authors
Lucy Maud Montgomery	Ray Cummings	Vaughan Kester
Luther Benson	Rex Beach	Victor Appleton
Lydia Miller Middleton	Rex E. Beach	Victor G. Durham
Lyndon Orr	Richard Harding Davis	Victoria Cross
M. Corvus	Richard Jefferies	Virginia Woolf
M. H. Adams	Richard Le Gallienne	Wadsworth Camp
Margaret E. Sangster	Robert Barr	Walter Camp
Margret Howth	Robert Frost	Walter Scott
Margaret Vandercook	Robert Gordon Anderson	Washington Irving
Margaret W. Hungerford	Robert L. Drake	Wilbur Lawton
Margret Penrose	Robert Lansing	Wilkie Collins
Maria Edgeworth	Robert Lynd	Willa Cather
Maria Thompson Daviess	Robert Michael Ballantyne	Willard F. Baker
Mariano Azuela	Robert W. Chambers	William Dean Howells
Marion Polk Angellotti	Rosa Nouchette Carey	William le Queux
Mark Overton	Rudyard Kipling	W. Makepeace Thackeray
Mark Twain	Saint Augustine	William W. Walter
Mary Austin	Samuel B. Allison	William Shakespeare
Mary Catherine Crowley	Samuel Hopkins Adams	Winston Churchill
Mary Cole	Sarah Bernhardt	Yei Theodora Ozaki
Mary Hastings Bradley	Sarah C. Hallowell	Yogi Ramacharaka
Mary Roberts Rinehart	Selma Lagerlof	Young E. Allison
Mary Rowlandson	Sherwood Anderson	Zane Grey
M. Wollstonecraft Shelley	Sigmund Freud	
Maud Lindsay	Standish O'Grady	
Max Beerbohm	Stanley Weyman	
Myra Kelly	Stella Benson	
Nathaniel Hawthrone	Stella M. Francis	
Nicolo Machiavelli	Stephen Crane	
O. F. Walton	Stewart Edward White	
Oscar Wilde	Stijn Streuvels	
Owen Johnson	Swami Abhedananda	
P.G. Wodehouse	Swami Parmananda	
Paul and Mabel Thorne	T. S. Ackland	